HAUNTED WORLD

HAUNTED HEARTS BOOK 2

SUZANA THOMPSON

ISBN 979-8298427883

CHAPTER 1

opened my eyes to an unfamiliar world. Ominous dark clouds drifted slowly across a bleak, gray sky. An eerie landscape of barren trees surrounded me.

Where was I?

The ground beneath me was hard and uncomfortable, covered sparsely by coarse, dry grass. I sat up, giving my aching back immediate relief. Standing up did the same for my sore butt. Why had I been lying on the ground? Had I passed out?

My head did feel a little fuzzy, but there were no bumps on it as far as I could tell after running my hands over it to check for injuries. I discovered that my hair was thick and silky, which seemed like a good combination. It hung past my shoulders and was a rich, chocolate brown.

Wait, why hadn't I known that already? And what about my eyes? Surely, I knew the color of my own eyes. But I didn't. And I didn't know what my face looked like either.

Nor my name, or anything about myself.

Panic made it hard to concentrate as I tried to recall anything at all about my life. I didn't know who I was or where I lived. How was I going to find my way home if I couldn't remember where it was?

Calm down, I told myself. Somebody would find me. If I wasn't home when I was supposed to be, then my family would come looking for me. They'd call the police if they had to.

But did I have a family? Why didn't I remember them? What if I was alone in the world?

It certainly felt that way. There wasn't another person around anywhere. I realized how still and silent everything was. No sounds of life—no car engines or voices. That didn't give me hope that there was a road nearby or a neighborhood with people.

Yet, shouldn't I at least hear birds or small animals scurrying around? There wasn't even the rustle of the wind. For a moment, I worried that I might be deaf, but clearing my throat produced a sound I could hear. So, that wasn't the problem. It was just dead air around me.

My heart seized in fear. Was I dead? Was this desolate place hell? But where were the demons? I glanced around in terror, expecting them to appear at any moment.

When that didn't happen, I came up with another explanation. Maybe I was in purgatory, some place between heaven and hell. But why was I here? What had I done to end up here alone?

Stop, I told myself. *You don't know anything yet.*

That was true. I couldn't allow myself to assume anything. There was no reason to think that I was dead. At least, not yet. What I needed to do was stick to what I knew—which was not much.

I snapped my fingers as I realized something. I had amnesia. That was a fact, and not a guess. I couldn't remember anything, so I had amnesia.

That made me feel better, because I thought it was unlikely I'd have amnesia if I had died. Wasn't the afterlife all about being rewarded for everything you'd done right, and paying for everything you'd done wrong? Part of that would have to be remembering what'd you'd done.

I liked this—coming to conclusions like a detective putting together clues. It gave me hope and helped me form a plan. I'd go in search of help, taking note of everything around me as I went so that I could describe my location to the police if I found a phone.

That spurred me to check my pockets, in case I had one on me. No such luck. Not only would it have been a way to call for help, but it would have given me information about the people in my life. I'd at least have known their names.

With a final look around me to make sure I hadn't dropped my phone on the ground, I spotted something strange. There was now a section of thick green grass beneath my feet. It spread out from me in a small circle surrounded by the dry, sparse grass I'd noticed before. Had that been there when I woke up? It stood out in such vibrant contrast to the drab colors around it that it was hard to believe I'd failed to see it. Yet what other explanation could there be? It hadn't magically grown in the few minutes I'd been standing there.

I gave up trying to figure it out and turned my attention to which direction I should go. There was a path nearby, which was helpful but still left me debating about which way was best. I couldn't stand here debating about it forever, so I chose randomly and started walking. As long as I stayed on the path, I shouldn't get lost. Which was a funny thought, since I didn't know where I was to begin with.

But a path meant people, right? I encountered no one as I followed the winding trail through the woods of barren trees with spindly branches reaching eerily up toward the gloomy sky. Finally, they gave way to an open field of dry, yellow grass. But what really caught my attention was the house. It was about thirty feet away from me, and it was three stories high. The top story had a tower room, and the bottom story had a porch that ran along the side. And the entire structure was gray. Gray!

Didn't the washed-out surroundings lack color already? Why would these people choose to paint their house gray amidst such a drab land-scape? Well, the only thing that mattered was if they had a phone I could use.

I trudged across the field in my white socks. Yes, I had no shoes on, which added to the weirdness of this whole thing. Had I left wherever I had been so fast that I hadn't had time to put on my shoes? Or had I been kidnapped?

That possibility hadn't occurred to me before, but now that it had, I looked warily at the house. What if my kidnapper lived there? What if I was walking into a trap?

On the other hand, why would my kidnapper leave me asleep in the woods? I had been completely defenseless in that state. But instead of being locked up, I'd been left free to wander anywhere I wanted and find help. No, the kidnapping scenario didn't fit my situation.

Feeling a bit more emboldened, I quickened my steps toward the house. As I neared it, I saw that I had to go around to the porch side to get to the door. The side facing me was all connected to the tower, and there were apparently tower rooms stacked on top of each other, so that each floor had one. I ignored the urge to explore such a cool structure and reminded myself that I was here in search of help.

Going around to the porch side, which was obviously the front entrance, I climbed up the stairs and knocked on the door. I waited and then knocked again, louder this time. When nobody answered, I pounded on the door and shouted, "Hello? Is anyone there? I need help!"

No response. Desperate, I turned the doorknob and pushed—and the door opened. It was unlocked! I cautiously peered inside and saw an empty entryway, seemingly faded of color just like everything else I'd seen since I woke up—except for the small patch of vibrant green grass I'd been standing on in the woods.

"Hello?" I called into the house. "Is anyone home?"

There was no answer, so I walked inside. I had to find a phone. If someone called the police on me for trespassing, it would be a relief at this point. The isolation was starting to get to me.

Yet there were no angry homeowners demanding to know what I was doing in their house. There was also no phone on the first floor. I hesitated at the bottom of the stairs, knowing that going upstairs would really be an invasion of privacy. That was where the bedrooms likely were. It was where people kept their personal belongings and things they didn't want to display to visitors.

It was also where someone might have forgotten their cell phone in the morning rush to get to work or school. That was probably wishful thinking, but I couldn't overlook the possibility.

I couldn't quite get myself to call out and announce my presence before I started up the faded wooden staircase. I was spooked by the silence and the abandoned feel of the place. But I noted that there was no dust on anything, so someone must live here.

The hallway at the top of the stairs led to three bedrooms and a bathroom, none of which contained a phone. Neither did the library, which was the turret room on this floor. I gazed at it in delight, thinking that it would be the perfect place to read with the light spilling in from the semi-circle of long windows surrounding the seating area. If only it was a brighter day.

That thought roused me from my pleasant interlude. How much time did I have before night fell? I hadn't seen a clock anywhere, which was weird. But maybe the people who lived here used their cell phones to tell time. They would have to, because there were no appliances displaying the time either. The kitchen stove was basic, with no digital display or buttons. There was no microwave, and I had seen no TVs anywhere and no game consoles. Maybe the family who lived here was Amish.

Yet that didn't fit either, because there were light switches in all the rooms. I flipped one, and the electric light came on in the library. I turned it off and continued on with my exploration by going upstairs to the third floor. Up here was the tower bedroom I wanted for myself.

The bed faced the windows, exactly as I would have placed it to enjoy the view. If there had been a better view. I drifted toward it to look out at the spooky world outside. From up here, I could see the barren trees I had come from stretching out into the distance. They really looked creepy from this perspective, and I was glad I had found my way out of them. Especially before dark.

Movement at the edge of my vision caught my eye, and I stared at the man riding a black horse through the field. He was approaching the house.

A person! There was a person coming here.

I sprinted out of the room and down the stairs in my haste to catch him before he left. Yanking open the door, I dashed out onto the porch just as he dismounted from the horse.

"Hazel, you're okay!" he exclaimed. "I wasn't sure if you'd ever recover. I can't believe you risked your life for him!"

"Uh, do you know me?" I asked.

It was a stupid question, since he apparently did. But I was having a hard time following what he was saying and needed him to slow down. I'd rushed out here to ask him for help, expecting him to be a stranger. Which he still was to me, because seeing him hadn't jogged my memory at all. Nothing about him was familiar to me.

I wondered how I could forget a face like that. He was the best-looking guy I'd ever seen in my life. Of course, I didn't actually know that, but I couldn't imagine anyone looking better than him. Not even with the frown he now wore.

"You don't remember me?"

"Don't be offended. I don't remember me either," I told him. "Or anything else. I have no idea who I am. But you said my name is Hazel?" I turned it over in my mind, trying to decide if I liked it.

His dark eyes narrowed on me. "If you don't remember anything, then how did you conjure this house?"

"I...what?" I asked in bewilderment.

He gestured behind me. "That house, Hazel. You thought I wouldn't know it didn't exist before? I know every inch of this place. This is *my* world."

I stared at him, my stomach sinking with dread. This guy wasn't going to help me. He was crazy, and I was here alone with him. Did he even know me? I now doubted everything he'd said, and I had a bad feeling that I was in real danger.

CHAPTER 2

backed up slowly, never taking my eyes off him. If he made any sudden movements, I'd dash into the house. Luckily, I'd left the door open in my hurry to run out here and talk to him. I hoped that I could get inside before he made it up the porch steps. Then I would lock him out and grab something to use as a weapon if he somehow managed to break in.

"I'm not going to hurt you," he said, sounding exasperated. "It's not my fault you jumped in front of him. You did that to yourself."

I had reached the doorway, while he hadn't moved from where he stood. There was no way he could get up here in time to stop me from fleeing into the house. Just as I was about to launch myself inside, I saw someone materialize beside him.

I blinked, but the person was still there—when no one had been there a second before.

"Hazel! Are you okay?"

It was the exact same person, except he was wearing different clothes. The one I had been talking to had on black pants and boots with a black button-down shirt, but several buttons were left undone, exposing his throat and some of his chest. It was a mix of formal and untamed.

The one who had just appeared was dressed in jeans and a white t-shirt with what looked like brand-new sneakers on his feet. He gazed at me with a concerned expression, and I immediately felt drawn to him.

But he had appeared out of thin air!

The first one sneered at him. "What are *you* doing here? Get out before I end your miserable life right now."

The second one was still focused on me. "Don't worry, Hazel. He can't keep you here. I'll help you get back."

I forgot my caution and hurried forward eagerly. "Do you know where I live? If you could tell the address to the police, that would be great. They should be here any minute," I lied, casting a quick glance at the first guy.

He snorted. "There are no police here, unless you conjured them too."

The second guy studied me with a puzzled expression. "You don't know your address?"

"I don't know anything," I told him, my frustration bubbling over. "I don't even know if I'm hallucinating you, because how could you just appear out of nowhere like that? But I don't care. Even if I am imagining you, I need you to tell me who I am and where I live. I just need some answers!"

"You have amnesia?" he asked.

"So she claims," the other one said. "Yet she apparently didn't forget how to use her abilities."

His twin continued to ignore him. "Your name is Hazel Guthrie, and you live in Salem, Massachusetts."

None of that sounded familiar, but it was nice to get some information about myself anyway. "Who are you?" I questioned. "How do you know me?"

"I'm Devon Culver, and I know you from school. We go to the same school and are in a couple of classes together."

"High school," I guessed, assessing his age.

"Yes," he confirmed.

"What a touching reunion," the other guy said sarcastically. "But you might want to get your beloved out of here before she's ripped to shreds."

Devon ran up the steps and threw himself in front of me, facing off against his twin. "You're not going to lay a finger on her. You take one step toward her, and I'll kill you!"

His doppelganger gave him a deadpan look. "*I'm* not going to hurt her, you idiot. But there are some nasty things here that come out at night."

I leaned to the side so I could see past Devon and look at him. "Who are you?"

His gaze shifted to me and turned thoughtful. "It seems I was mistaken. You apparently *do* have amnesia. I suppose it's not surprising, given that your foolish heroics put you in a coma. You're fortunate to have survived at all."

I gaped at him, taking a full step to the side so that I was out from the protection of Devon's body. "I was in a coma?"

"You still are," Devon said, half-turning to look at me. "That asshole's right about one thing: you need to get back and wake up."

I stared at him. "Are you crazy too? How can I be standing here talking to you if I'm in a coma?"

"He's not crazy," the other guy said. "He's a pathetic waste of space, but not crazy." He cast a glance at him. "Oh, by the way, how does it feel to walk again?"

Devon froze and looked down at his legs, slowly looking up again with a thunderstruck expression on his face.

His twin regarded him with grudging approval. "You were so busy saving Hazel that you didn't notice. I suppose you can give yourself a pat on the back for returning the favor and leaping in front of her—now that you can leap."

"I'm healed?" Devon asked in wonder.

His mirror image laughed. "Sure. Go back to your body and get up."

Disappointment replaced the amazed look on Devon's face. "It's only while I'm here."

"What are you guys talking about?" I demanded in exasperation. "I don't understand your twin language, so explain everything to me so I can know what the hell is going on."

"He is not my twin!" Devon exclaimed.

I glanced back and forth between them, double checking that they looked identical. "Then who is he?"

A smirk formed on the guy's lips before he answered. "My name is Braxton."

Devon was down the porch steps in a flash and in his face. "Don't you dare speak my brother's name, you evil asshole. You're not worthy to even say his name."

Unperturbed, his doppelganger remarked, "It seems that Hazel isn't the only one suffering from memory loss. You've obviously forgotten some things about your brother if you've put him on a pedestal. I know it isn't polite to speak ill of the dead, but—"

"Shut up!" Devon shouted. "Shut your fucking mouth!"

The other guy grinned. "Touchy subject. But he was the one who found the grimoire, so you have that to thank him for."

He sidestepped Devon and focused his attention on me. "Okay, then. As flattered as I was to know that you called me Sexy Devon in your mind, I think it would hurt Devon's fragile feelings to hear you call me that out loud. So, I'll pick another name that suits me —Lucius."

Devon snorted. "More like Lucifer."

"Why are you picking a random name?" I asked. "What's your real name?"

"It's not random," he told me. "It was my ancestor's name, Lucius Culver, and it's been my name my entire life."

"You mean five years?" Devon said derisively.

"I've accomplished more in those five years than you have," Lucius shot back.

"Oh yeah? Like what? Tricking Hazel into feeling sorry for you?"

"She actually does feel sorry for *you*, so you've got me there. I had to pretend to be pathetic for her to feel sorry for *me*," Lucius taunted back.

"Hey, guys," I interrupted, because something beyond them had caught my attention. "What is that?"

Lucius turned to look behind him at what I was pointing at.

Darkness was creeping in over the trees. The light wasn't fading into darkness like normal when night was approaching. Instead, the darkness was already there, and it was spreading over the land like a shadow, engulfing everything in its path. My heart pounded in fear as it slowly crept toward us.

Lucius sprinted up the porch steps, and I thought he was going to take shelter in the house with us. Before I knew what was happening, he'd scooped me up and ran back down with me.

"Hey!" Devon protested and hurried after us.

But Lucius had already hefted me onto his horse and hopped up behind me. I screeched and held on to the raised part of the saddle, shoving my feet into the stirrups so I wouldn't fall off—effectively helping him kidnap me as we galloped away. Devon just missed us as we took off.

Despite the fact that Lucius had ambushed me, I felt the urgency of our escape. "What about Devon? We need to help him!"

"Your house might protect him."

"Might? What if it doesn't? We have to go back for him," I insisted.

"Nobody told him to come here in the first place. He's on his own, just like I was. My only concern is keeping you safe."

I was glad that my safety was a priority for him, but I hated that he didn't care about Devon being in danger. "What's going to happen to him? What's out there?"

"Out here," he said and banded his arm across my waist in a tight hold as he urged the horse into a breakneck speed.

We raced over the flat, barren ground like the hounds of hell were on our heels. My heart pounded as fast as the horse's hooves as terror stole my breath. His solid body pressed against mine, but we were out in the open. Could he protect me from whatever lurked in the darkness? I shuddered as I recalled his words about being ripped to shreds.

"You're safe with me," he spoke into my ear. "No matter what happens, you're safe with me. Don't try to run away."

I hoped that I wouldn't. I wanted to be brave and defend him if he was overpowered by the thing in the dark. But I would probably run away screaming.

"You're safe with me," he repeated. "No matter what it looks like, you're safe with me."

That had me imagining a hideous monster. On some level, I knew that monsters weren't supposed to exist. Even with my amnesia, I knew that much. But darkness wasn't supposed to creep over the land like that either. I didn't dare look back to see if it was catching up to us.

What would happen when it did? We couldn't outrun it forever. It would eventually reach us.

My fear intensified when I spotted a wall of fog in front of us. It stood there like a dividing line between the faded light on this side and the dense, impenetrable gray that hid the unknown on the other side. It was just as unnatural as the creeping dark behind us. What was waiting for us in there?

"Lucius," I said urgently as we sped toward it. I wasn't sure what I was warning him about, because we clearly had nowhere else to go.

"We're almost there," he said.

That reassured me that the fog wasn't a danger, but I still braced myself as we crossed into it. Despite how solid it had looked, we went through it like it wasn't even there. On this side, it was like ordinary fog.

Lucius slowed the horse to a trot, and my fear spiked again. Seeming to sense this, he said, "It's okay. We're safe now."

"You're saying the wall of fog can keep it out?" I asked dubiously.

"It's protected. Nothing can get through unless I let it."

That sounded about as believable as me conjuring a house, but I'd seen several unbelievable things—including Devon appearing out of thin air. So, I kept my doubts to myself and hoped that he was right about us being safe.

I could barely see a few feet in front of us, but it was more of the same flat, barren landscape. At least it was easy for the horse to travel over, but I wondered how long it could keep going before it got tired. Maybe we should stop and give it a break now that we were supposedly safe.

I gasped as a castle came into view before us. A castle!

It was massive, with towers and turrets, and even a drawbridge though there was no moat to cross. The horse's hooves clattered on the wood planks as we trotted over it. The gate opened as if by magic as we approached, and we entered a courtyard and halted.

Lucius dismounted and reached up to help me down. I stood on shaky legs and stared at him. "You live in a castle?"

He smirked, dropping his serious expression for the first time. "I had to make do until I could take my rightful place as the heir to the Culver fortune."

"But you're already rich if you have a castle! Are you some kind of prince? And what country is..."

I trailed off as something struck me. "Wait, isn't Devon's last name

Culver? Are you guys related? He said you're not his twin, but are you cousins?"

Could cousins look exactly the same? Maybe there were subtle differences that I hadn't noticed in my state of confusion and fear.

His smirk now seemed to be suppressing a laugh. "Cousins, yes."

Unsure if I believed his answer, I accepted it for now. "I really hope he's okay."

His expression soured. "Your amnesia hasn't cured you of your obsession with him. What will it take for you to come to your senses?"

"I'm not obsessed, I'm worried," I argued. "Like any normal person would be. The question is, why aren't you? Don't you care if he gets hurt? He's *your* cousin. You should be even more worried about him than I am!"

"He'll be fine," he said impatiently. "Come inside and get some rest."

He began to stride toward the castle, but I quickly called out, "What about your horse? Shouldn't he be in a stable?"

Halting in his tracks, he turned and strode to the horse, who was still standing patiently in the same spot.

"What's his name?" I asked, admiring the beautiful creature.

"Diablo."

I frowned as I watched him unfasten the saddle. "That sounds familiar."

"It means devil in Spanish," he said.

My frown deepened. "Why would you give him a name like that? I would have called him Midnight."

He gave me a sharp look. "Are you sure you don't remember anything?"

I perked up at that, hoping that I had subconsciously remembered something. "Why? Do I have a horse named Midnight?"

His expression lost its hard edge. "No. I suppose it's a common name for a black horse. It's not surprising you would choose it."

He dropped the saddle on the ground, and Diablo circled around us and took off at a sprint in the direction we had come from. My anxiety spiked as his hooves clattered over the drawbridge.

"Stop him," I pleaded. "He's going back out there!"

"Yes," Lucius confirmed to my horror. "He wants to run free."

"But it'll get him!" I still didn't know what *it* was, but I knew it was bad.

"No, it won't. He belongs out there."

"What are you talking about?" I questioned. "You said we were in danger out there. Don't you care what happens to your horse? And what about food and water for him? There's nothing out there except dry grass."

"No, I said *you* were in danger out there. Nothing out there can harm me anymore. And Diablo has always been a part of the darkness. He serves me because I mastered him, but I let him be wild and free the rest of the time. As for food and water, he needs none. But you do. Come with me," he said and pivoted, striding off.

"Of course, he needs food and water," I argued, hurrying after him.

But he ignored my complaints, even as he held the wooden door open behind him so I could follow him into the castle. He clomped across the stone floor in his boots, drowning out the sound of my footsteps as I walked in my socks. I wondered again why I had no shoes on.

My eyes wandered over the dim entry hall, lit only by an ornate standing candelabra and several smaller ones ensconced along the walls. On the left, a wide staircase curved up out of sight, while a hallway up ahead led deeper into the castle. We went that way and entered a huge dining hall with a long table that reminded me of a scene from the first Harry Potter movie.

Except that we were the only ones here. There were no other people here to greet us. Yet there was a feast set out at the head of the table, covered by silver serving lids—but no servants.

How had they known to expect us and when to prepare the meal? I hadn't seen Lucius call anyone since he'd been in my presence. Had he just assumed before he left that I'd be coming back with him?

There were two place settings set out, so he had to have been expecting another person to join him. How had he known that I would? And where was his family?

"Where is everyone?"

He pulled out a chair and gestured for me to take it. "Milady."

I played along as I sat down, because he was being so charming and polite—and we were in a castle! "Thank you, Milord."

His smile brightened his dark eyes as he gazed down at me, and it made him even more attractive. "You'll have fine dresses to wear," he told me. "And jewels to adorn your beauty."

His lovely words only made me aware of how much I didn't fit into this setting. I was dressed in a t-shirt and sweatpants like I was supposed to be lounging around the house—not dining in a castle. And I was sure that my socks were dirty from walking around outside in them. Attired to meet royalty I was not.

"Where is everyone?" I asked again.

The smile slipped off his handsome face. "There's no one else here."

I glanced at the covered dishes on the table. "You mean they all went home?" My gaze shifted back to him, and my stomach sank at the hard expression he now directed at me.

"I mean I've all you've got, so you better learn to appreciate it. This is my world, and I am lord and master here. Don't look for anyone else, because there is no one. Your precious Devon is probably gone by now too, so you're alone with me."

CHAPTER 3

awoke in my comfortable bed, thinking that it had all been a dream. A hot guy who appeared out of thin air, creeping darkness, and castles. Of course it hadn't been real.

But when I opened my eyes, I saw that I was in a room with stone walls and arched windows showing a gray world outside. Thick, ornate columns supported the wooden canopy above me. I slipped out of the bed fit for royalty and gazed up at the candelabra chandelier hanging from the ceiling.

There was no denying that I was still in the castle, and that it hadn't been a dream. Which meant that I was alone here with Lucius.

But that couldn't be true. He couldn't take care of a place this big all by himself. I glanced around and saw that there was no dust on the armoire and no cobwebs on the chandelier. He must have maids who cleaned these rooms, even if they didn't live here. Someone had to have cooked and set out the meal I had been too upset to eat last night.

Had it been night? The foggy view out the window was the same now as it had been before I went to sleep. Surely night had fallen at some point. I could tell that I had slept for many hours, because I was so well rested.

I glanced at the bed and froze. The vivid purple comforter stood out from the brown wood of the frame. Except it had been white when I had pulled it aside to get beneath it and lay down on the sheets, which were also white. But they were now purple too.

I would have suspected Lucius of sneaking in here and switching the comforter to mess with me, but he couldn't have switched out the sheets without waking me up. Not unless he'd drugged me. That would have been impossible for him to do since I hadn't eaten or drank anything he had offered me. I'd only had water from the faucet in the bathroom.

It had been a relief to see that the castle had indoor plumbing. I'd read a few historical romances, and I sure didn't want to go to the bathroom in a chamber pot. And it was nice to have my own private bathroom. I wondered if I had that at home. My memory still hadn't returned, and I felt really lost without it.

But how could I remember books I'd read when I couldn't remember my life? How did I know what a chamber pot was but not where I lived? I knew about modern conveniences but no personal details about myself. It was bizarre, and so was this entire situation.

I went into the bathroom, making sure to lock the door behind me. I didn't trust Lucius to respect my privacy. He had to have somehow changed the bedding while I slept. What other explanation could there be? It hadn't magically transformed into a different color.

I looked around the bathroom and spotted the towel right away. It was the one I had used to dry my hands after I washed them. It had been brown then. It was now purple. All the folded towels were still the same drab brown as this one had previously been.

What kind of game was Lucius playing? Why would he come in here and switch out one towel?

I took note that everything else was the same. A brown towel hung neatly over the white, claw foot tub. The white basin sink rested atop a wooden platform, with pipes running beneath it into the stone floor.

My eyes moved up to the mirror on the wall and held on my image. I'd studied my features last night, seeing that my eyes were brown and that my face was a girl next door kind of pretty. I wasn't a stunning beauty, but I wasn't bad either.

That wasn't what held my attention now. It was what I could see of the nightgown I was wearing. It had been laid out on the bed when Lucius had brought me to the room. And it had been white like the comforter beneath it. Now it was a pale pink.

I looked down at myself to confirm the color, and anger began to boil within me.

How dare he!

My face burned with the heat of humiliation as I thought about him undressing me. All I had on beneath this were my bra and panties. So, he'd seen me practically naked.

I fumed as I used the toilet and washed my hands. Ignoring the purple towel out of spite, I grabbed one of the folded brown towels to dry my hands. I saw in the mirror that my hair was sleep mussed, but I didn't care. I wasn't trying to look pretty for that creep. Which was also why I changed back into my sweatpants and t-shirt rather than putting on one of the dresses he had shown me were in the armoire.

I flung the bedroom door open and marched out into the hallway, only to be stopped short by the sight of Lucius walking toward me.

"Good, you're awake," he said. "Breakfast is ready."

Humiliation and rage warred within me as I gave him a death stare. "How dare you touch me!" My voice came out shaky, and I was mortified that I sounded like I was about to cry.

He halted and regarded me with annoyance. "I grabbed you to keep you from being ripped apart. I didn't have time to ask you politely to get on the horse."

"I'm not talking about that! You changed me into a different nightgown. Who does that? What the hell is wrong with you?"

Confusion crossed his face. "A different nightgown?"

I pivoted and stalked back into the room, pointing to it on the floor. "This one. Don't pretend like you don't know."

He entered and looked from the nightgown to the bed, and then he stared at me with a look of wonder. "How did you do it?"

I was thrown by his question and his demeanor. I had expected denials and gaslighting about how I hadn't remembered the color correctly.

He continued. "I've never been able to bring color into this world, no matter how much power and control I've gained. But you've done it in one day. How?"

He was still gazing at me in amazement, but my frustration with him erupted. "What are you talking about? I want to know why you undressed me!"

He blinked, coming out of his state of wonder. "You think that I..."

His offended expression morphed into a hard look. "Come with me," he commanded and strode out of the room.

I rushed after him, incensed that he thought he could end the argument without explaining himself. Stomping down the stairs behind him wasn't satisfying, because I didn't have shoes on to make noise. I had changed my dirty white socks out for a woolen gray pair that had been in the armoire.

Lucius led me into the same dining room we'd been in yesterday and yanked out the chair I'd briefly sat in. "Look," he demanded.

I saw it immediately. The cushioned seat, which had been a cream color, was now a vivid purple.

"Hazel, you did this," he said. "I thought it was just this one object, but you changed the color of your nightgown and all the bedding. And you did it without even knowing it," he marveled. "I've been trying for years with no success."

I was back to suspecting that he was crazy. "That's because you can't magically change what color something is. You have to dye it another color if you want to do that."

"Then how do you explain this?" he challenged, gesturing to the chair. "And your nightgown and sheets and comforter?"

"You did it," I said, although I was less sure of that now. "You changed them all out for different ones."

"Without waking you?" he asked in disbelief.

"You must have drugged me," I said, although I knew I was grasping at straws at this point.

"Why?"

I looked at him, reluctant to speak my answer aloud. When I did, it came out sounding like a question. "Because you're a pervert?"

Anger sparked in his dark eyes, and his jaw hardened. "Tell me this then. If that's the case, why would I alert you to it? Why wouldn't I leave everything the same so you would have no knowledge of anything being amiss?"

He had me there. I couldn't think of a reason for him to make it so obvious.

"I'll leave you to your breakfast," he said curtly and strode past me.

"Wait, aren't you going to eat?"

He kept going as he replied, "And be accused of leering at you throughout the meal? I think not, milady."

He left the room, and I felt bad for driving him away. But what was I supposed to think? His claim that I had done it myself defied logic. It wasn't possible.

But hadn't I seen several impossible things since I had found myself in this strange world? I thought about Devon appearing out of thin air, and the darkness creeping over the land. Was it any more fantastical for some fabrics to magically change color?

I could only think of three explanations. I could be crazy and hallucinating all of this. That made a lot of sense, because besides all the impossible things happening, there was also a castle. Why would there be a castle when I obviously wasn't royalty? But did crazy people know they were crazy?

What would make the most sense was this all being a dream. Anything could happen in a dream, so nothing was impossible. But it didn't jump around from scene to scene like dreams usually did. Time was moving at a normal pace, and everyday things like going to the bathroom were also happening. And when was I going to wake up?

The last explanation was the hardest to believe: that this was all real. It would mean that magic existed. That thought triggered a memory of Lucius mentioning a grimoire to Devon. Wasn't a grimoire a book of spells?

An odd excitement unfurled in my belly as I started to open my mind to the possibility of magic being real.

And I was hungry. It wasn't just excited butterflies in my stomach. It was a sharp hunger pang too. I had no idea how long it had been since I'd eaten, but I couldn't resist the delicious smell of food for another minute.

Just like last night, there were two place settings across from each other at the end of the long table. Between them were serving platters hidden beneath silver covers. I removed one of the lids and saw a row of crisp bacon. Grabbing a piece, I took a bite and quickly devoured the whole thing as I looked at what was under each lid. There were scrambled eggs, sausage, waffles, and biscuits. A small serving dish held butter. An entire gravy boat was full of syrup.

I put some of everything on my plate and poured myself a glass of milk from one of the silver pitchers. The other one was filled with water. The only thing lacking was gravy for the sausage and biscuits, but I wasn't complaining. They tasted great without it too.

Sitting on my pretty purple chair, I ate until I was stuffed. Then I started to feel bad for Lucius. Was he waiting for me to leave the room so he could eat? There was a lot of food left, and I had covered it back up with the lids after taking how much I wanted. It should still be warm.

But what about Devon? Was there any food in that house? I'd seen a refrigerator but hadn't looked inside it.

More importantly, was Devon okay? What if he was hurt and needed help? I couldn't bring myself to consider the worst-case scenario. He was alive. He had to be.

Maybe he had teleported himself out of danger just as quickly as he'd appeared before my eyes. Of course he would use his ability to save himself. Relief flooded through me.

And I realized that I had accepted that this was real. Because I wasn't just seeing it with my eyes. I was experiencing it with all my senses. I'd smelled the food and tasted it. The wooden table in front of me was solid to the touch. I knocked on it and heard the sound. It was all tangible and real.

Which meant that I needed to deal with the situation I was in and learn as much as I could about it. Standing up decisively, I looked down at the cushioned seat of the chair. Had I really changed the color of it? If so, then how? Lucius hadn't known either. He'd been awed by it, but it was a little underwhelming for me as far as magical powers went.

I'd much rather have the ability to teleport. Now that was a cool power! And much more useful.

I needed to talk to Devon. He might know how to explain how my ability worked. I also wanted to know that he was okay.

First, I had to find Lucius and ask him if he could take me back to the house. I went out into the hallway and called his name, hoping that he was nearby. There was no response, so I searched the rooms for him.

When I saw the kitchen, I took a moment to look around. There was no stove, and I wondered if they actually cooked all the food in the pots hanging over the fireplace. The fireplace that looked cold and unused.

I frowned as I put my hand above the clearly unburned logs and felt no heat. Where had they cooked the breakfast I'd just eaten? And where were they?

I hurried back to the dining room in case they were already clearing the table, but it sat untouched. My steps hastened as I went down the hallway and poked my head into each room, looking for people.

Lucius's words from last night were in my head, but they couldn't be true. He wasn't here alone. There had to be someone else here.

But I found no one on the first floor. Going up to the second, I made a quick stop in my room to wash my hands, because I could still smell the bacon on them. This time, I dried them with the purple towel. Now that I wasn't freaked out by it, I did like seeing the splash of color. It was a bright spot in this place, although the white bathtub and sink were nice too.

I discovered that Lucius's bedroom was at the end of the hall in the opposite direction of the staircase. There was another hallway here which was much longer and appeared to be going across the entire castle. I couldn't see an end to it from where I stood.

"Lucius?" I called out as I stepped into his room.

My bed was big, but his was even bigger. It sat on a raised wooden platform with an arched structure held up by wide, fancy posts, like he was truly a king. There was even a chandelier hanging right above his bed. It looked like a room within a room, made just to keep his royal bed in. There was enough space on the platform for a person to stand comfortably beside the bed, and I stepped up onto it.

Placing my hand on his white comforter, I closed my eyes and pictured it turning a royal blue. After a moment, I looked and was disappointed to see that it hadn't changed color.

With a sigh, I stepped down from the platform and left his bedroom. Moving down the long hallway, I glanced into the open doorway of each room I passed but didn't linger. I called out his name at intervals but got no response.

What was more disturbing was that I encountered no one else in any of the rooms. There was not one person anywhere. I began to fear that Lucius had abandoned me, and that I was completely alone here.

To my immense relief, I heard music as I approached the end of that long hallway. Hauntingly beautiful music that evoked sadness and long-ing. My heart ached as I listened to it, even though I didn't know what I was longing for. Whatever it was, I couldn't remember it. Yet I felt it in my soul.

The sound emanated from another open doorway, but this one led into a huge ballroom. The man at the piano drew my eyes across the expanse of the empty dance floor.

It was Lucius who was playing this exquisitely heartbreaking music.

How could I have suspected him of anything bad when he could play with such deep emotion? I was on the verge of tears by the time he finished.

He sat for a beat after the last note, and then he shifted his body on the bench to look at me, like he had sensed me standing there.

Our gazes locked, and I had a disorienting feeling of déjà vu.

CHAPTER 4

"Hazel!" Lucius exclaimed as I swayed on my feet.

He shot up out of his seat and hurried toward me, but I was back to normal by the time he reached me.

"It's gone," I told him. "I almost remembered something, but it's gone."

It had involved him. Staring into his eyes had triggered an intense feeling that I had experienced this before. I tried to get it back by gazing intently at him, but it didn't work. Had it been the music? But it had happened after he stopped playing.

His mouth flattened into an unhappy line before he spoke. "You need to remember and go back to your life. You don't belong here."

"Where is here?" I asked. "Are we still in America? Because Devon said that I live in Massachusetts. Is that where we are?"

"No," he replied in a flat tone.

"Europe?" I guessed. Because I thought they had castles in Europe.

"No."

His one-word answer frustrated me. "Then where are we?"

He expelled a breath. "I don't know."

I gave him a deadpan look.

"It's true," he insisted. "This is where I found myself when Devon banished me."

"Banished you?" I questioned.

"That's right, you don't remember any of that. It's not important now. The point is that I'm not sure what this place is. I thought it was hell at first, but it can't be because I've become its master. And I know I'm not the devil," he added with a wry smile.

Before I could process that, he said, "Also, there aren't any other people here. I doubt that hell would exist just for me."

That should have had me scoffing in disbelief, but my mind was putting together all the bizarre clues that wouldn't let me dismiss his words so easily. There were no phones or TVs. Not just in this castle, but in the house where I'd sought help.

During our trek here, I hadn't seen any cars, or even any roads. Or another person.

Except for Devon.

"I want to go back to the house," I declared.

His expression hardened. "No."

Annoyance chased away the warmth I felt toward him after hearing him play. "Who are you, my father? I can go if I want to. If you won't help me, I'll get there by myself."

"You can't," he stated like it was a fact.

"Watch me," I snapped and spun around to march out of the room.

I heard his unhurried footsteps behind me, which reminded me that I still didn't have shoes. But I couldn't worry about that now. I had to get back to that house and find other people.

Because we couldn't be the only ones here. That was too terrifying of a thought, and I refused to believe it. I held on to the knowledge that Devon had been there. Lucius had talked to him too, so I hadn't hallucinated him.

And someone had to live in that house. It hadn't looked abandoned, so that was proof that there were more people.

Lucius just didn't want me to go check on Devon, because he hated him for some reason. Well, I didn't care, because I was going. Besides wanting to make sure that he was okay, I needed to find my way home. I was hoping that seeing my family and where I lived would make me remember who I was.

Lucius followed me down the long hallway back to where our rooms were. I kept going past them and down the stairs. He said nothing as he walked behind me through the castle and out the door into the courtyard.

The place was still shrouded in fog, and I wondered when it would clear. Lucius's boots clomped on the cobblestones, highlighting the silence surrounding us. He didn't stop me from walking out of the open gate and onto the drawbridge. His footsteps thudded on the wood as we crossed it.

I looked around for Diablo but didn't see him. It would have been nice to borrow him, but I couldn't ask when Lucius was being so rude and unreasonable about me leaving. I'd just have to make my journey on foot.

Except that my foot hit something, and I stopped with my toes smarting with a dull pain. I searched the ground in front of me for the object I had stumbled into, but there was nothing. Cautiously, I took tiny steps forward, still looking down until I bumped my head into something. I lifted it to see what was there, but I saw nothing but fog.

I slowly raised my hands and moved them forward until they touched something solid. It felt like a wall, and I ran my hands over it, up and down, and then to the sides as far as I could reach. It was there right in front of me, but I couldn't see it.

I realized that I had to be at the place where we had crossed over into the fog yesterday. It had looked like a wall of fog from the other side, but it hadn't been solid at all. We'd passed through it with no resistance.

I dropped my hands and made a slow turn to face Lucius. He stood about six feet away watching me with his arms crossed casually and one foot crossed over the other so that he held all his weight on one strong leg. His expression was ever so calm and patient.

It filled me with dread. Because he obviously knew that I was trapped here. He'd just come to watch me discover that for myself. "What did you do?" I asked, my voice trembling with both fear and awe. Because how could he make an invisible wall?

"I told you. Nothing can get in or out unless I allow it."

"So, you're keeping me prisoner here?" I demanded. "That's kidnapping! Let me go right now, or you'll get arrested."

He straightened from his casual pose, uncrossing his arms and standing firmly on both feet. His expression turned serious too. "I'm keeping you here for your own safety. You have no knowledge of the dangers of this world or how to fight them. And no one will arrest me. There is no police force here. There are no people at all."

He had to be lying. Because there were always people. I didn't remember my life, but I knew that society existed. Devon had mentioned going to school with me, and that meant teachers and students. Which meant that there hadn't been an apocalypse that wiped out humanity.

Which meant that Lucius was lying to me.

As if to prove my point, a girl's voice called out, "Hazel! Hazel, where are you? Hazel—ouch! What the hell?"

She was behind the invisible wall, but I couldn't see her. She'd probably bumped into it like I had. More importantly, she was looking for me.

"I'm here!" I shouted.

"Hazel! I hear you! But how do I get to you? I can't get through this fog."

I turned to Lucius with a pleading look. "Please let her in."

He heaved a sigh and then said, "Tell her to come in."

"But you didn't do anything," I protested.

With an annoyed look at me, he called out, "You can pass through now."

The girl had more faith in him than I did, because she stepped into view as I turned to look. Happiness lit up her pretty face as soon as she saw me. "Hazel!" she exclaimed and threw her arms around me.

I hugged her back awkwardly, not wanting to be rude, but also feeling uncomfortable because she was a stranger to me. Extricating myself as soon as I could, I stepped back to regain my personal space. "So, you know me?"

Her mouth opened in surprise before her gaze moved past me and narrowed. "What did you do to her?"

"Who are *you*?" Lucius demanded.

"I'm her best friend, and I want to know why she doesn't know who I am. What did you do—besides put her in a coma? That's right, I know it was you," she added, her blue eyes blazing with anger. "You're that guy she was talking to. I knew you were a demon!"

"What?" I exclaimed and whirled to stare at him in horror.

He looked up as if for divine intervention and then leveled an irritated look on the girl. "I'm not a demon."

"That's what a demon would say!"

He sighed. "You are a tiresome person. What are you doing here?"

She puffed herself up, adorably trying to look bigger and stronger than she was. "I came to take Hazel back, and you're not going to stop me."

He nodded. "She needs to go back."

"But you wouldn't let me leave," I reminded him. "You put up a wall to keep me here."

"I meant that you need to go back to your world," he snapped. "I can't have you wandering around mine. It's too dangerous for you."

Since I now had another person who was apparently on my side, I felt safer to tell him what I thought. "Do you know how crazy you sound right now? Your world and my world? We live in the same world! I might have amnesia, but I know that we all live on earth."

"Actually, I don't know where we are" the girl said. "But, Hazel, your body is in the hospital. You're in a coma."

I looked at her like she was crazy too. "How can I be in a coma when I'm standing right here?"

She shook her head. "I don't know, but you are. I saw you lying in that hospital bed, and I tried talking to you, but it didn't make a difference. Your parents are in shock. They found you passed out on the floor in your room, and they couldn't wake you up. Nobody could figure out what happened to you, but I knew." Her gaze shifted to Lucius and hardened. "I knew it had to be him."

I had parents who cared about me. I had hoped that I did, but it was nice to hear this girl confirm it. "What's your name?" I finally asked.

"Oh!" she exclaimed with a wide-eyed expression as she turned her attention back to me. "I'm Abby. Gosh, it's so weird that you don't know that. We've been friends since kindergarten."

"This is all very touching," Lucius said sarcastically. "But perhaps you can reunite on your own time in your own world."

Abby threw a glare at him before saying, "Sounds good to me. Let's go back, Hazel."

"Okay," I agreed eagerly. "But how do we get there?"

She took off the backpack she was wearing and unzipped it to pull out a thick, leatherbound book. When she opened it, she cried out in dismay. "It's blank! What happened to the writing? Oh my God, all the spells are gone!"

The panic on her face as she flipped through the empty pages spiked my own anxiety. I hadn't entirely believed her claim that I was in a coma, but the promise of a family had sounded wonderful. Now my hopes of returning to my life were crumbling again.

"How did you get your hands on the Culver's grimoire?" Lucius demanded.

"It was in Devon's room," she answered distractedly. "What are we gonna do? We can't get back!"

He expelled a heavy, exasperated breath. "Come with me. I have a copy of it." He turned and strode off, expecting us to follow.

Abby hurried after him. "Oh, thank God! I thought we were stuck here."

She'd apparently forgotten that she'd accused him of being a demon just a few minutes ago. I caught up to her and walked beside her. She glanced at me and smiled, and she radiated so much warmth and affection that I knew she was telling the truth about us being friends.

"I'm so glad you're okay. It was awful seeing you in that hospital bed and not being able to wake you up."

"I still don't understand how I can be there and here at the same time," I told her.

But she was no longer listening to me. Her steps slowed as she stared straight ahead. "It's...is that a castle?"

"Yeah, that's where Lucius lives."

She stopped and gaped at me. "He lives in a castle? Is he a prince?"

I shrugged. "He didn't tell me."

"Didn't you ask? That would have been my first question. I mean, who else lives in a castle?"

"He sure thinks he's royalty," I commented drily. "You should see his bed. Five people could probably sleep in it. It's that big, and it's up on this platform like he's too important to have it on the floor."

Her blue eyes widened even more. "You slept in his bed?"

"No!" I quickly corrected her. "He gave me my own room."

"Girls! Chat later. Time is of the essence, and we must seize this opportunity while we can. Quickly now," Lucius said and did two sharp hand claps to get us going.

It worked, but I wondered why he was in such a rush now when he'd been sitting and playing his piano until I found him in the ballroom. He hadn't been worried about time then.

"It's amazing how he looks exactly like Devon," Abby said as we walked across the drawbridge. "Except for not being in a wheelchair. Is he really his twin?"

I glanced at her. "Why would he be in a wheelchair?"

"I keep forgetting that you don't remember any of this stuff. Devon is a guy from school, and he looks exactly like him." She gestured toward Lucius. "Except he's in a wheelchair."

I was the one to stop in my tracks this time. "Devon is in a wheelchair? Oh my God! What happened? I knew we shouldn't have left him there alone!"

She waved away my concern. "Oh, he was in an accident a long time ago. But you've seen him? He's here?"

"A long time ago? But I saw him yesterday, and he wasn't in a wheelchair."

She gaped at me. "He's been healed? How?"

An idea formed in my mind as I thought about my nightgown and bedding changing color overnight. Maybe I didn't have magical powers. "Maybe this place is magic."

Abby's face lit up with excitement. "I had to use a spell to get here, and that's magic, right? And it healed Devon! That's amazing. I'm so happy for him!"

"Girls!"

"C'mon," I said and marched into the courtyard and up to Lucius.

"This is Abby," I told him. "And Abby, this is your gracious host, Lucius," I added, hoping that my sarcasm wasn't lost on him. "Now you know her name, and you already know mine, so you can stop calling us girls like we're in elementary school."

"Apologies milady. Forgive my lack of manners. I wasn't aware that I was being rude to an uninvited guest who appeared without warning and demanded entry."

He turned his attention to Abby. "Milady," he said with a formal bow. "Welcome to my home."

Despite his less than welcoming words about her arrival, Abby swooned a little at his medieval gentleman routine. "Thank you."

Before she could say more, he turned and strode to the door, and we followed him into the castle. Abby gazed around at everything like we were on a sightseeing tour. I could tell that she wanted to stop and explore every room that we passed, but Lucius kept a quick pace as he led us to the third floor.

We entered a massive room that made us both gasp. It was like stepping into space and being surrounded by hundreds of dazzling stars. They weren't just on the ceiling like in a planetarium. They were all around us too, like brilliant jewels suspended in the air. I cautiously reached out to touch one, but my hand encountered nothing. It illuminated my hand when it passed through it, so it was some kind of light.

The rest of the room was dark, and the floor was black. But the stars were so bright that we had no trouble seeing where we were going. We walked a distance that seemed like it spanned the length of the entire castle. The room wasn't just long but enormously wide too, stretching out in both directions from us. I could easily believe that it took up the entire third floor.

The space and stars appeared endless, but Lucius opened a door up ahead that revealed a lit room. It was an office with an antique writing table in the center, upon which was a leather book. Long, tall windows let in the natural light from the foggy world outside. I'd forgotten that it was daytime after being surrounded by darkness and stars.

"What kind of projector was that?" Abby asked. "I've seen the ones that project lights onto houses for Christmas, but nothing that looks like real stars. I know it probably costs a lot, but I haven't even heard of movie stars using something like that. Is it something new?"

"No, it's something old. I assume you used the spirit walking spell to get here?"

She grimaced. "Um, I don't remember what it was called. Devon had it open to that page, and I said it while I was picturing Hazel. I know there was a part that went what is lost now is found."

"Ah, of course." He opened his book and turned the pages until he found the one he wanted. "This should work to get you back as well. You'll need to envision yourself instead of Hazel, but it will be effortless. Your spirit will naturally be drawn back to your body."

"Oh good," Abby said in relief. "I was a little worried about that, since I couldn't get Devon to wake up either." She winced. "I probably should have told his dad, but I knew I wouldn't be able to try the spell if I did that. I was going to hurry and get it done, and then get help for him."

"It's okay," I consoled her. "We'll all be home soon."

"And you need to stay there. Both of you were lucky that you arrived here during the day. If it had been night, you wouldn't have fared so well. So, don't come back—ever."

"What was in the darkness?" I asked. "What were we running away from?"

He shook his head. "You don't need to know. Suffice it to say that it is the stuff of nightmares."

"Are you saying it's a monster?" Abby exclaimed. She glanced at the windows in fear, like something out in the fog was about to crash through to get us.

"More than one," Lucius said. "So, make sure you stay safely in your world."

She stared at him in horror. "What about you? You need to get out of here too! No wonder you were asking Hazel to help you."

"Thank you for your concern, but I'm safe here. They can't cross the barrier outside. Nothing can without my permission."

"The invisible wall, right," she said. "It's good that you have that."

"But it wouldn't have been good for you if we hadn't been out there to hear you." He gestured toward her blank spell book. "Without a way to get back, you would have been stranded out there until dark. Alone and helpless."

She shivered. "I didn't know it was dangerous." Looking at me, she added, "But it was worth it to get Hazel back."

My heart warmed with the realization that I had a true friend. That was followed quickly by a stab of guilt for what I was about to do. I wanted to warn her not to come looking for me again, but I couldn't give myself away in front of Lucius.

Luckily, he did it for me. "Remember, don't come back. You won't be so fortunate next time."

"We won't," Abby assured him.

Lucius shifted his gaze to me, and I nodded. "Thank you for helping me."

His dark eyes brightened. "Of course, milady."

Then he was back to business. "Now, as I said, each of you will picture yourself as you recite the spell." He turned the book so that it was facing us and we could read it.

Abby took hold of my hand, which made me worry that we would be linked and end up in the same place. But then I remembered that she had said I was in the hospital, and she was in Devon's room. We were about to be parted regardless of where I went.

I gave her hand a little squeeze, hoping that she would heed Lucius's warning and not come looking for me again.

CHAPTER 5

could feel Lucius's eyes on me, but I blocked him out as I pictured Devon instead. He had a different kind of energy about him, and not just because he was wearing jeans and a t-shirt. I'd been drawn to him, and I let that guide me as I envisioned him by the house where I'd seen him. Abby and I read the words aloud together.

"Bound and binding
    Binding bound
    See the sight
    Hear the sound
    What was lost
    Now is found
    Bound and binding
    Binding bound
    Keeper of what disappears
    Hear me now, open your divine ears
    What is lost, I now wish to find
    Help me stop being blind
    Direct me to what I seek

By fire, air, earth, and sea"

Nothing seemed to happen as I finished reciting the spell and stared at the words on the page. But I blinked, and I was no longer in that room. I was outside, but not in the fog. Weak sunlight showed me a path of vivid green grass in the field of dried grass I'd walked through to get to the house. It hadn't been there yesterday, but I didn't waste time wondering how it could have grown so fast.

Turning, I saw another strange thing. Each porch step had one area where the wood looked brand new. It was a rich brown, but it was part of the original board, which was a faded, weathered brown. I had walked up those steps right where the fresh wood was, and I had walked over the grass that was now green. Could I really be doing this without even knowing it?

But I had more important things to focus on right now. "Devon," I called out.

I went up the porch steps and knocked on the door. "Devon, it's Hazel. Are you here?"

Maybe he had gone home. But then why had I been transported here when I had pictured him during the spell? I turned the knob and opened the door. Unlocked, which was another sign that he probably wasn't here. Wouldn't he have locked the door to keep out the monsters? I would have barricaded it too.

My heart almost stopped when I stepped inside and saw him. He lay bloodied on the couch, with gashes ripped into his clothes and flesh. "Devon!"

His eyes fluttered open, and I rushed to him. "Oh my God! We need to get you to the hospital."

"Hazel," he said in a strained voice, "you have to get out of here."

"We both do. I've memorized the spell. I've got to write it down before I forget it. Hold on."

I raced through the house, opening drawers in search of a pen and paper. I found them in a bedroom upstairs. They weren't where I thought they'd be. The old-fashioned desk was cool, but it was empty. In desperation, I looked inside all the dresser drawers and discovered that the bottom one held a leather-bound book and pens. There was no loose paper, so I took out the book.

As soon as I picked it up, I knew that it was mine. I held it for a moment, trying to summon a memory that confirmed my overwhelming feeling that it belonged to me. Was it a family heirloom that had been passed down to me? It looked old. Or had I bought it at a garage sale?

I opened it and was startled to see that Hazel's Book of Spells was handwritten on the first page. I tried to recall writing it, but my mind was frustratingly blank. And I was wasting time when Devon urgently needed help.

I flipped through it, searching for a blank page. Finding a few at the end, I wrote down the spell I had used to get here. Once that was done, I focused on something niggling at the back of my mind. Had I seen the word healing as I was flipping through the pages?

I went back to the beginning and turned them more slowly until I came across it again. After reading it, I took a candle and box of matches out of the drawer as well and carried everything downstairs.

The sight of Devon's injuries shocked me again. The slashes ran the length of his entire body, from his chest and arms to his legs. I didn't know how deep they were, but I worried about how much blood he'd lost. His eyes were closed again, and I wasn't sure if he'd fallen asleep or passed out. I didn't disturb him, wanting him to conserve his energy.

Opening the book to the correct page, I set it down on the coffee table and knelt in front of it. I lit the candle and held it as I read the spell aloud.

"Burn the sickness in your flame
    Burn the sickness that would maim
    Burn the illness by your might
    Burn the illness in your light
    Heal him of illness or pain
    And heal him of all that is bane
    Heal him and set him free
    With my will, so must it be"

· · ·

As I spoke the words, I pictured his gashes closing up and his scars fading into unbroken skin. I recited it three times in case I needed to say it more than once. Closing my eyes, I focused extra hard on envisioning Devon the way he'd been when I saw him yesterday.

"Hazel."

My heart leapt at the sound of his voice. It was stronger, and I squinted one eye open to take a peek at him and see if the spell had helped. To my amazement, he was sitting up. His alert eyes showed no trace of discomfort or pain, although he was still bloodied.

"They didn't get you," he said, looking me over.

"What are they?" I asked. "And why didn't you go back to get away from them?"

"The spell," I said, answering my own question. "You didn't have the spell."

He stood up and dug into the back pocket of his tattered jeans, pulling out a piece of paper. It was intact, so I assumed he'd been attacked from the front. He handed it to me, and I saw the spell I had memorized written on it.

"That was smart. Abby should have copied it down too and brought it with her."

"Abby is here?" he asked in alarm. "Where is she?"

"She's back home," I reassured him, hoping that was true.

A look of relief crossed his face before an urgent expression replaced it. "We have to get out of here too—before they come back."

Cold dread ran down my spine. "Yes, let's go now. Lucius told me how to do it. You need to picture yourself when you say the spell. I pictured you to get here, and it worked."

"So that's how you escaped from him," he mused to himself. His eyes took on a hard edge as they fixed on me. "What did he do to you?"

"Nothing!" I exclaimed quickly, because he looked like he was about to go murder Lucius. "He took me to his castle. Can you believe he lives in a castle? And he had dinner ready for me, but I didn't eat it because I thought it might be drugged or poisoned. But then I was too hungry not to eat breakfast, but it was good. But anyway, I wanted to go see if you were okay, but he wouldn't let me. Not until Abby showed up, and I lied to him that I was going home with her."

He stared at me.

"Sorry, that was a lot. The point is, he didn't do anything to me."

His dark eyes searched mine until he appeared satisfied that I was telling the truth. My stomach fluttered as we gazed at each other.

But then his expression became stern. "Why didn't you go home? Why would you come back here instead of escaping? Don't you have any sense at all?"

That stung, especially since I'd thought we were having a moment, and that he'd been feeling it too. "I came to help you."

"I don't need your help. I can take care of myself."

"Yeah, I can see that," I shot back sarcastically. "You were doing great bleeding to death."

He glared at me. "I would have been fine. I just needed to rest for a while."

I let my eyes trail over his countless wounds and blood-soaked clothes, and then gave him a pointed look. He was either in denial or being a stubborn idiot. And he was ungrateful.

"You healed me," he said, without an iota of thanks in his tone. "Now go home."

I was so done with him! "Fine, I will."

Folding his sheet of paper into how he'd had it before he took it out of his pocket, I threw it at him. He caught it, and I huffed and flipped to the back pages of the spell book and found the one I'd written the spell on.

This time, I pictured myself in a hospital bed as I spoke the magic words. When I was done, I stared at the page as I waited to be transported there. I blinked, but nothing happened. Closing my eyes, I willed myself to that place. But when I opened them, I was still in the same room.

"What are you doing? Go home."

"I'm trying!" I exclaimed. "It's not working."

"You probably remembered it wrong. Here, use this one," he said, handing me the paper back. "I copied it exactly from the grimoire."

As I unfolded it, I could tell at a glance that the words were the same. But I recited them anyway as I focused extra hard on envisioning myself in that hospital room.

But it didn't make any difference. I was stuck here.

CHAPTER 6

Fighting the panic clawing at my insides, I told myself that it was just temporary. "I probably used up too much…"

Too much what? Magic? Maybe it could be depleted. But then how was it replenished? There was so much I didn't know about how this all worked.

"You probably can't use the same spell twice in one day. I'll try again tomorrow."

Devon looked close to panicked himself. "You can't be here tonight. You've got to go home before it gets dark."

"I can't! It's not working!"

"Try again," he insisted.

So, I did. Three more times before I admitted defeat. "You go," I told him. "Save yourself."

"I'm not leaving you here alone. I'll protect you," he said with grim determination.

Considering the state I'd found him in, all he'd do was delay my demise by getting himself killed first. We needed a better plan than that. "Maybe there's a protection spell in here."

I started at the beginning of the book and began to turn the pages. "Here's one!"

He walked over to my side of the coffee table and looked down at it. When he glanced at me, I saw the skeptical look in his eyes.

"The healing spell worked," I reminded him, noticing that blood wasn't seeping from his wounds anymore. I couldn't tell what they looked like beneath the old blood that was drying over them. I hoped they were healing okay, and that they wouldn't get infected.

"Can you sit down here beside me? Or should I move to the couch? I think we should do this spell together, so it will hopefully be more powerful."

He lowered himself to the floor with ease. The fluttering in my stomach started up immediately with his nearness. It was ridiculous since we were about to cast a spell, not play spin the bottle.

And I didn't need that thought in my head.

"Um, okay, I'll light the candle. Because, uh, maybe it helped with the healing spell." God, I sounded as nervous as I felt.

He lit the candle and handed it to me. Fixing a fierce look on me, he said, "We can do this, Hazel."

The unspoken part was that we had to. Or we might not make it to see another day. I fought my rising panic, because what if the healing spell had used up the last of my magic? Nothing had worked after that. What if this didn't either?

The touch of Devon's hand jolted me, both with startling me and with shooting an electric spark through me. The butterflies were back, and they had brought friends. My gaze met his, and I was sure that he felt it too.

He swallowed and looked away toward the book. Clearing his throat, he asked, "Ready?"

Right, the spell. I shifted my gaze to it, but I was still extremely aware of Devon holding my hand. My body buzzed with excitement and anticipation.

And latent power. I could feel it through our connection, and I gripped his hand harder, trying to tap into it as I answered, "Ready."

We began to recite the words in the book.

"Gods above and gods below
Protect this home from wicked foe

Elements water, earth, air, and fire
Harbor this home from thief and liar
Ancestors ancient and old
Defend this home from hearts of cold
Spirits from beyond the misty veil of silver
Safeguard this home from vile pilferer"

Silence settled over us after we spoke the last word. My mind slowly shifted from imagining an impenetrable force field around the house to the fact that Devon was still holding my hand. I turned my head and caught his gaze.

Time slowed as my heart stopped.

The moment stretched back in time to a memory that was just out of reach. But I knew that this had happened before. I'd stared into his eyes and been thunderstruck. It wasn't much to go on, and it slipped away as the here and now hijacked all my attention.

My heartbeat stuttered and then sped up. The air between us became charged with electric anticipation as we stared at each other.

Devon let go of my hand and abruptly stood up. "I'm going to see if I can find some clothes and take a shower."

A wave of embarrassment swept over me. Had I really been expecting him to kiss me? We'd only been holding hands because of the spell, and I'd turned it into some romantic fantasy. I hoped he hadn't noticed, but the sudden awkwardness between us told me that he might have.

"Uh, yeah, that's a good idea," I said in a lame attempt to save face.

He made his escape from my presence by going upstairs. Watching him walk away in his blood-stained and shredded clothes brought back the reality of the situation we were in.

What if the spell didn't work? I realized that we wouldn't know until it was put to the test. I sprang up and went to look anxiously out the window. No creeping darkness yet, but I didn't know how much time we had. I hurried to lock the front door before rushing to check that the back door was locked as well. They were solid wooden doors, but could they hold out whatever was out there? I'd have to get Devon to help me barricade them with some furniture.

But what about the windows? Glass was more easily broken through than wood. That thought had me going in search of weapons. I found metal fireplace pokers and some knives in the kitchen. Hardly adequate protection, but better than nothing.

Maybe there was a spell we could use to defeat our enemies. I picked up the book and sat down on the couch to flip through it. Most of it was about the use of herbs to treat various illnesses. So, basically, old folk remedies. There were some love potions and some spells for divining the future. Also, the various powers of crystals. But no spells to fight monsters.

I did find another protection spell, and I wanted to use it for extra insurance. The more protection, the better. We couldn't have too much in my opinion.

I also said a prayer to God. I had no idea if I believed in Him, but I figured it couldn't hurt to appeal to Him too.

I then paced anxiously around the room, keeping a vigilant eye on the windows. So far, it was still bleak and gray outside.

Devon came downstairs dressed in pinstripe gray suit pants and a white button-down shirt with a wide collar that was perfectly pressed and folded over. But he had left the top buttons undone, exposing his throat and just a peek at his chest. Which revealed unbroken skin with no wounds. The long sleeves were rolled up, showing forearms which also had no wounds.

I gaped at him, remembering the bloody gashes across his arms. They had been clearly visible since he had been wearing a t-shirt. Now there weren't even any scars. It was all smooth, unmarred skin—like he had never been injured at all.

"These were the only clothes I could find," he said. "It's all suits that look like they're from the 1940's."

He obviously misunderstood why I was staring at him. "You're healed," I marveled. "You're completely healed."

He looked down at his legs and then glanced up at me. "Oh, you mean the cuts from their claws."

Icy dread ran down my spine, but I had noticed his subconscious tell and took the opportunity to ask about it. "Abby said that you used to be in a wheelchair."

He had been inspecting his arms, but his gaze snapped back to me. "I was. What do you think about that?"

"I think it's great that you can walk again! You must be so happy!"

His expression dimmed, and I got the sense that I had said something wrong. "Right. Of course that's what you want."

"Don't you?" I asked in confusion. "I would think you'd be thrilled."

He scowled. "I would be."

Before I could ponder that statement, he inclined his head toward the pile of knives and fireplace pokers. "Why'd you throw those on the floor?"

"I didn't throw them. I set them there so we'd have weapons. Also, we should push the couch in front of the door."

He nodded, but his expression revealed that he thought all my efforts were useless.

"And there's another protection spell," I added in desperation. "Let's do it right now."

We did the same thing as before, sitting next to each other on the floor, with me holding the lit candle. But this time I was too anxious to pay much attention to his proximity to me. I was aware of time ticking down, even though there weren't any clocks in this house.

"Craft this spell in the fire
    Craft it well, weave it higher
    Weave it now of shining flame
    None shall come to hurt or maim
    None shall pass this fiery wall
    None shall pass, no none at all"

Once again, I had no idea if the spell would work. So, we pushed the couch in front of the door, and wedged the kitchen table against the back door.

Devon almost lost his balance, and I rushed to steady him. "What's wrong?"

He stumbled against me, almost knocking me over before shooting out a hand to grab the counter top. "Must be the blood loss. Plus, I haven't had anything to eat or drink since I got here."

"Hold on. I'll get you a chair." I carefully slipped out from under his arm, guiding that hand to grip the counter too.

Quickly dragging a chair over to him, I helped him sit down. Finding a glass in one of the kitchen cabinets, I filled it with water from the faucet and handed it to him. He gulped it down in one go and set it on the counter beside him.

I opened the old-fashioned refrigerator and discovered shelves stacked with Tupperware containers. There was also a plate of fried chicken covered by plastic wrap. I pulled it out and put a drumstick on an empty plate for Devon. He set it on the counter and grabbed the drumstick to devour without worrying about crumbs falling onto his clothes or on the floor.

"I wonder who made this food," I said as I opened a container and saw potato salad inside it. Rummaging around until I found the cutlery drawer, I took a spoon and scooped some out onto Devon's plate and set a fork out for him to eat it with. I also gave him another drumstick, since he was already done with the first one.

"I don't know, but it's really good," he said. "Can I have some more water?"

I poured him another glass, which he also drank down fast. This time, he picked up the plate and held it as he ate, showing that he'd gotten some of his strength back. Maybe he'd been dehydrated, because I doubted the food would have had that quick of an effect on him. I filled his glass again, but he was now more focused on his meal.

"Aren't you going to eat?" he asked.

"I'm not hungry yet," I answered, and tried not to think about the possibility that I might not get the chance to eat later. What if this was my last chance to taste food? But my stomach was too tied up in knots to even consider it.

"I'll be right back," I said and hurried back to the living room to look out the window. Seeing that nothing had changed outside offered very little relief. I knew that the darkness would be coming for us.

"We should go upstairs," I heard Devon say. "The bathroom doesn't have any windows. I think that's our best bet."

I turned to see him standing several feet away. "Is that what you did last night? Is that how you survived?"

He snorted. "I was an idiot last night. I was furious that asshole kidnapped you right in front of me, and I went around the house looking for a garage and some kind of vehicle I could use to go after you. They attacked me from behind before I even knew what was happening."

"They?" I asked as dread slid down my spine. I quickly moved on before he could answer. "But how did you get away from them?"

"I didn't. They left me for dead. I must have passed out from the pain, and maybe they thought I was dead or it wasn't fun for them anymore. Anyway, it was daylight when I woke up, and they were gone. I was somehow able to crawl into the house through the back door and get to the couch."

I stared at him in horror. "Fun for them?"

But his gaze had moved past me. "Get upstairs now!"

I turned to look and saw the darkness creeping over the trees in the distance. I yelped when Devon grabbed my arm, startled in my terror, even though I knew the monsters weren't in the house yet. He tugged me into motion, stopping only so we could grab our weapons off the floor. Then we were rushing up the stairs, with him letting me go first but then leading the way once we were on the second floor.

He entered a bedroom walked through it to a bathroom and flipped on the light inside it. As he had said, there were no windows. I dumped the knives I was carrying into the bathtub, but I held on to the fireplace poker and walked over to the bedroom window.

CHAPTER 7

"What are you doing?" Devon demanded. "We need to get inside the bathroom."

But he came to stand beside me and watch the eerie darkness creep over the trees and start spreading over the open field of mostly dry grass in front of the house. My heart pounded in fear, but I had to see it coming and know where it was at.

Devon apparently felt the same way, because he stood there watching it with me.

"We'll go in the bathroom if we have to," I assured him. "Maybe the spells will work."

I realized that I had just revealed my doubt to him, but I couldn't fake confidence right now. Not while I watched the darkness reach out with tendrils like it was a living thing and creep forward toward the house. It was like being trapped in a nightmare.

Devon offered what comfort he could as he took my hand in his warm, strong one. We stood united as the darkness crept over both earth and sky. It extinguished the weak daylight but replaced it with a blood red moon. I blinked as I saw it in the sky. When had it appeared? It was big and not easy to miss.

Devon sucked in a breath, drawing my attention to him. He stared out the window with wide-eyed terror, and my heart seized in fear as I followed his gaze to what was on the ground below us.

Two pale creatures crawled on limbs that were disproportionately long to their compact bodies. They were almost spider-like, but they had humanoid type arms with hands that had sharp claws instead of fingers. Instead of legs, their hind limbs were the same, so it looked like they had four long arms. Humanoid heads protruded from their bodies, but the faces were straight from a nightmare. Gaping open mouths that were black holes with nothing inside. And white eyes staring out of their pale faces.

Terror held me in its grip as they crept closer, and I tightened my hold on Devon's hand. He was frozen beside me, probably reliving his horrible encounter with them. I knew that I should get him to the bathroom and away from the sight of them, but I had to know if they could get into the house.

The very thought of it made me want to scream and run away in panic. I didn't know how Devon had survived them on his own yesterday. Imagining him outside with those things with no one to help him had me shuddering in revulsion and horror.

I held my breath as they crawled closer to the house—and then came to a dead stop. They tried to move forward and were halted again like they'd hit an invisible force field. Barely daring to believe that the protection spells were working, I waited in tense silence to see what would happen now.

In unison, the creatures looked up at our window like they knew we were there. I stumbled back, but Devon held his ground.

"Looks like it's working," he said.

I had the irrational fear that he would jinx us by saying that, but I reminded myself that Lucius had said that nothing could get through his wall of fog, and nothing had. He must have been using some kind of protection spell too.

Movement down below caught my eye, and I froze in terror. More monsters were coming to join the first two—and they were approaching from both sides of the house. Meaning that they had surrounded the house and been trying to get in from every side. We wouldn't have seen them coming if they had succeeded, because we had been focused on the two on this side.

Now they were all gathering together. I counted thirteen in total, and the superstitions about that number were not lost on me. Superstitions about bad luck weren't so easy to dismiss when you were facing monsters, which weren't supposed to be real either.

They swarmed together and started attacking the invisible field holding them back. They were trying to break through by combining their strength in an attempt to weaken our shield. My heart leapt into my throat every time they surged toward it.

They were relentless and tireless, going at it like a battering ram. It was holding for now, but how long could it withstand them? I prayed to God to save us, because I didn't know how we'd be able to fight off so many vicious creatures. Could our weapons even hurt them? They didn't appear to be sustaining any injuries from repeatedly slamming into the barrier keeping them out. If it was anything like the one Lucius had, then it felt like a solid wall. But they kept hitting into it without hesitation, and without any damage to themselves.

Did they not feel pain? Were they invincible? What if we couldn't fight them off? Would I even be able to fight, or would I be paralyzed in fear seeing those horrible things coming at me?

"What if they get in?" I couldn't stop myself from saying the words aloud. Devon didn't need that thought in his head, but he had to be thinking it too, regardless if I said it or not.

He turned to look at me, and I was surprised by the fierceness in his eyes. "I'll fight them, Hazel. They only got the jump on me last time because I didn't know they were coming. But I'm strong here, and I can protect you."

His confidence gave me courage. "We'll fight together." I still desperately hoped that we wouldn't have to.

He let go of my hand and gestured toward the bed. "Get some rest. I'll keep watch."

I glanced at the monsters outside and shook my head. "I can't sleep. You lay down, and I'll keep watch."

He sighed and pulled a chair covered in ugly upholstery over to the window. "You can sit and keep watch."

I gestured to the other chair. "Bring that one here too, and take a break. You don't have to actually stand guard. We'll have time to get to the bathroom if we have to."

"I'd rather stand, but you go ahead and sit."

"C'mon," I urged. "You don't have to do the protective guy thing. In fact, you should save your strength, since you were injured."

His gaze dropped from mine. "It's not that. I just, uh, like standing. Anyway, you healed my injuries. They're all gone."

I was about to argue with him when it hit me. He wasn't lying about wanting to stand and being secretly macho. With everything that was happening, it had slipped my mind that Abby had told me he was in a wheelchair until he came here. I'd revel in standing too if I hadn't been able to do it for years.

"I can't believe I forgot!" I exclaimed. "Abby told me about you being in a wheelchair, and now you're healed! I'm so happy for you!"

He looked at me, and I was taken aback by his flat expression. "Of course you are."

I'd obviously said the wrong thing, but I didn't know what. Maybe it wasn't me though, because he'd also been surly after the healing spell. Instead of thanking me, he'd claimed that he hadn't needed my help. He was so moody and confusing!

I turned away from him and went to sit stiffly in the chair, aware of the awkward tension in the room even as I kept a careful watch on the monsters outside.

The silence stretched on until I couldn't stand it any longer. "Tell me about my life," I requested. Surely, I couldn't offend him with questions about myself.

"I'm not sure I should. I don't want to give you false memories."

"False memories?" I questioned.

"Yes," he said, his voice sounding closer as he replied. "You might start to picture the things I tell you about. Then you might begin to think that you remember them when you really don't."

He was standing close now. I could hear his voice above me and feel his presence right behind me. It felt intimate in the semi-dark, with only the light from the bathroom further behind us spilling into the room. The monsters outside seemed surreal at this point, but Devon was very real, and I was very aware of him.

I kept my eyes on the window, afraid that he'd retreat from me if I turned to look at him. "You told me we went to school together, and I didn't get any false memories from that. Even though I tried to picture it in my mind."

"That's because you didn't have the right picture," he said flatly.

I knew that he was referring to being in a wheelchair, and I quickly steered clear of that. "I couldn't picture my parents either. Even seeing Abby didn't bring back any memories, and she said that she's my best friend."

"I think you need to go home to get your memories back."

"You're probably right. I'll try again tomorrow."

Yet it troubled me that the protection spells had apparently worked, but the spell to go home hadn't. That meant that I hadn't used up the magic I was allotted for one day. That particular spell just hadn't worked. But it had worked to bring me to Devon.

Because he was still here in this world. But it hadn't worked when I had tried to go to my world. Was I stuck here?

I looked out at the hideous monsters in horror. Was I trapped here with them for the rest of my life?

CHAPTER 8

The darkness left the same way it had arrived, except in reverse. We watched it creep backwards, revealing a gray sky and a barren landscape as it retreated. The red moon disappeared in the blink of an eye and was replaced by weak sunlight. But it was enough to drive away the monsters, which was all that mattered.

I got up from my chair and collapsed on the bed in exhaustion. Devon stood up from the other chair, having eventually succumbed to taking a seat after standing for a long time. "I'll go lay down too, and I'll be back to wake you in four hours."

"Okay," I said, already closing my eyes.

I knew nothing else until I became aware of a warm hand on my arm gently shaking me. "Hazel. Hazel, wake up."

My eyes opened to the sight of Devon's gorgeous face. "Sorry," he said, "but it's been four hours."

I hoped that I didn't look like a mess, but I refrained from patting down my hair. He didn't know that I cared about what he thought about my appearance. My focus shifted to what he had just said as it registered in my mind. "You found a clock in your room?"

"No." He pulled a phone out of his pocket. "I used this."

I brightened and exclaimed without thinking, "You have a phone? Call someone to come get us!"

"Uh," he said carefully, "did you forget where we are? We're not in Salem or anywhere with people. To be honest, I don't know where we are. Also," he added with a sheepish expression, "I checked, and I don't have a signal."

I found his embarrassment endearing, and it helped alleviate mine. "I would have checked too, just in case. And like you said, we don't know where we are."

"Well, wherever we are, we need to get home before it gets dark again."

I sat up in alarm, and swung my legs over the side of the bed to get up. "Oh my God! Yes, we have to go!"

He put out his hand to stay me. "Don't panic. It's only been four hours since dawn, so we have time."

But I was eager to leave right away and rushed past him. "C'mon, let's go."

He followed me out into the hallway and downstairs to the living room. The couch was still blocking the front door, so I sat down on the floor and flipped through the spell book on the coffee table.

Devon sat down beside me, and my stomach did that fluttering thing again. I ignored it and said, "Maybe we should hold hands." Instantly, my face heated. "For the spell! Abby and I did, and it worked."

He took my hand, and I felt an electric zing at his touch. My gaze caught his, and we stared at each other until he looked away. "Okay, tell me when you're ready."

I struggled against my feelings of rejection and refocused on the spell and my desire to get out of here. Picturing myself in a hospital bed, I stated, "Ready."

We recited the spell together and waited, but nothing happened.

"Damn it," Devon said, expelling a breath. He let go of my hand and stood up. "Maybe you need some food to get your strength back."

He strode away toward the kitchen, and I got up and followed him. When he stopped dead in his tracks, I bumped into him. "Sorry!"

"What the hell?"

I was about to apologize again, but he stepped into the kitchen. As he moved out of my line of sight, I saw that the table was back where it had been before we used it to barricade the back door. And it was set with two plates of Belgian waffles and two glasses of what looked like milk.

"Oh my gosh, I was craving waffles!" I exclaimed as I rushed into the room.

Devon walked over to the table and touched one of the waffles. "It's warm." He glanced around. "Who the hell made these?"

I grabbed the butter knife and began to slather butter from the dish which was also conveniently set out. "Who cares? They look delicious."

"Hazel, those could be poisoned."

I picked up the glass pitcher of what looked like syrup and poured it over my buttered waffles. "That's what I was worried about at Lucius's castle, but the food was fine. And you ate the food from the fridge yesterday," I reminded him.

"Yes, but this is freshly made. Which means that someone was just here. So, who was it, and where are they?" He glanced at the stove. "What did they cook it in? There aren't any pans or even bowls in the sink from the batter." He gestured at the countertop. "And no toaster, even though these are clearly not frozen waffles."

He was right, and there was also no dishwasher where they could have stashed the dirty dishes they had used to make the waffles. I recalled that there had been no explanation to how the food had been made at the castle either. It had just been there on the table, like our breakfast was now.

I hated to say it, because it sounded absurd. But I could think of nothing else to explain it. "I think it's magic."

He scoffed, like I knew he would. "Magic waffles?"

I sat down and picked up my knife and fork. "I'm not letting mine get cold. You do what you want."

He eyed me in disapproval as I cut a piece and brought it to my mouth. It tasted as good as it looked, and I ate a few more pieces before taking a sip of the cold, refreshing milk. By this time, Devon had joined me and had already finished off one of his waffles even though he'd gotten a later start.

Between bites, I told him about the food at the castle and the lack of servants to cook it and serve it. And about how there hadn't been any sign of anyone using the kitchen to prepare the meal, exactly as we'd noticed here.

"So, you think it appeared by magic," Devon said.

My shoulders lifted in a shrug. "I mean, we used magic to protect us from the monsters. And I used magic to get here from the castle. And you and Abby used magic to get here, right?"

"Okay, magic is real," he acknowledged. "But who used it to make us breakfast? You can assume that it was him at the castle, but he's not here with us. He wouldn't be hiding if he was."

He was right about that. I hadn't known Lucius long, but I already knew that he wasn't a person who hid from anything. He might leave if he got upset or angry, but he didn't hide.

"We're the only other two people here," Devon pointed out. "I didn't do it, and neither did you. So, who did? And who moved the table back?"

I hesitated as a thought occurred to me.

"What?" he asked. "Who is it?"

I grimaced, reluctant to voice my crazy idea. "Um, well, something weird happened when I was at the castle. My sheets and my nightgown changed color overnight. And so did a towel I had touched and a chair I'd sat on. I thought Lucius had done it, but he was all excited about it and asked me how I'd done it. But I didn't know I had. I wasn't sure what to think, but the grass outside is green now, and I think it's the part I walked on. And I was craving waffles, so maybe...it was me?"

Devon stared at me for a second before scraping his chair against the floor as he got up. "It's out front?"

I realized he meant the grass, but he was already striding in that direction before I could answer. Scooting my chair back, I hopped up and hurried after him. He began to pull the couch away from the door, and I sprinted over to help him. When there was enough room to open it, he unlocked the door and went outside.

The trail of green grass was visible from the porch, and he stopped in his tracks. He then slowly descended the steps to walk over to it. Crouching down, he grabbed a fistful and rubbed it between his fingers. Letting go of it, he inspected his hand as he stood. "It's not paint."

He looked at me as I walked up beside him. "And it was all dry grass when I arrived yesterday. This grew overnight."

"Yeah," I agreed. "I noticed that too. It wasn't like this when I walked out of the woods and found the house."

He turned to fully face me. "If you're doing this without even trying, then you should be able to make the spell work if you focus. You should easily be able to get back to Salem."

"I tried! Don't you think I want to get out of here? I don't want to be here when those monsters come back."

"Well, something is keeping you from leaving. Do you think it's *him*?"

"No," I said. "Lucius told me to leave with Abby. He even warned us not to come back."

Devon expelled a frustrated breath. "Then it has to be you keeping yourself from leaving. Some kind of mental block."

I couldn't believe he was blaming me for being stuck here, and I lashed out at him. "Oh, yeah? And what about you? Why are you still here? What kind of mental block do *you* have? Abby was able to get back, so why weren't you, huh?"

He fixed that flat look on me that cut me down more than his anger ever could. "I wasn't trying to leave. I'm not going anywhere until I know that you've escaped this place. I'm not leaving you here alone with those things."

Despite his attitude, I couldn't help feeling grateful. Being here by myself with the monsters would have been so much worse. I didn't know how I would have made it through without him. "Thank you," I said sincerely. "I know that I should tell you to go and save yourself, but I'm not that brave. I'm really glad you're here."

He scoffed at my gratitude. "You're here because of me. I could say that you're here because of your own stupidity, because you threw yourself in front of me to save my life. But ultimately, it's my fault for creating him in the first place. It doesn't matter that it wasn't intentional. I'm responsible for all of this."

There was so much to process in that statement that I didn't know where to start first. "What do you mean you created him? You're talking about Lucius?"

"If that's what you want to call him."

"Whatever," I said, refusing to get sidetracked by things that didn't matter. His name wasn't the important thing. "How did you create him? How is that possible?"

The answer came to me immediately. It was the same way any of this was possible—lush grass growing overnight, objects changing color without being dyed or painted, and being able to change locations by reciting a spell. "Magic. You used magic."

He nodded with a grim expression.

"But then why do you hate him? And why does he hate you? He wouldn't exist without you, right? So, he should be thanking you."

He snorted. "Well, he's not. In fact, he wants me dead so he can take over my life."

I tried not to let my skepticism show on my face, but he must have seen it, because he barked out a harsh laugh. "You don't believe me. The irony."

"It's just that, he hasn't done anything bad. He treated me like a guest at his castle, and he let Abby in and helped us leave. And he played this beautiful music on the piano with so much emotion." I couldn't imagine a murderer doing that.

"So, because he doesn't act like a cartoon villain, you think he's a good guy? Next, you'll be getting into cars with strangers who offer you candy."

I put my hands on my hips, ready to let him have it. "I didn't leave with him on purpose. I'm not stupid! I was mad at him for kidnapping me, and—"

"Oh, so you know you were kidnapped? With the blinders you have on, I thought you would see it as a heroic act of chivalry."

I glared at him. "Since we're talking about blinders, let's talk about yours. Lucius might not be a good guy, but he's not as bad as you're making him out to be. I don't see him here trying to murder you."

My words struck him hard, and I thought I was getting through to him as a look of realization dawned on his face. "You're right. He's got the advantage on me here, so why isn't he using it?"

The blood drained from his face. "Because he thinks I'm already dead. He assumed those monsters killed me."

"But they didn't," I said, not understanding why he was so upset. "You're okay. You said yourself that all your wounds are healed."

The bleak look in his eyes held no hope. "He's done it. He's stolen my body."

CHAPTER 9

"What?" I asked, completely perplexed. "How could someone steal your body? That's not possible."

He looked out across the barren landscape. "I'm stuck here."

"Devon!" I snapped at him to get his attention.

His gaze shifted to me, and I spoke in a calm and reasonable tone. "Nobody can be in your body but you. That's what you're talking about, right? Him possessing your body?"

Unease skittered down my spine as I said that. Possession was such a creepy concept.

"Yes," he confirmed. "That's what I was talking about, and he can do it."

"But how? You said he did it because he thinks you're dead, but you're not. So how can he take your body if you're alive?"

"Because I'm not in it. I'm here instead. That gave him the perfect chance to steal it away from me."

"You don't know that," I said. "You're just assuming all of this, but you haven't even tried to go back to your body. You've got to do that right now."

I could see that he wanted to, but he shook his head. "I'm not leaving you here alone."

Hardening my resolve, I insisted, "I'll be fine. I'm the one who saved *you*, when you think about it, with that healing spell."

Intensity burned away the bleak look in his eyes. "You did save me. That's why you're in a coma, Hazel. Because you risked your own life to save mine. You almost *died* because of me."

I stared at him, processing what he was saying and trying to remember it. But there was nothing except the stirring of the butterflies in my belly because of his intense gaze. The girl in the coma was far away and hard to reconcile as being me. I was right here, right now—with Devon.

A drop of water splashed on my face, and I looked up at the gloomy sky as more raindrops fell. I raised my arms and delighted in the gentle shower of rain. Devon smiled as he watched me, allowing himself to get soaked too.

"I love the rain!" I decided aloud.

He laughed. "I can see that." Swiping a hand over his dripping face, he said. "I'm going inside to get dried off."

Still smiling, he turned and walked back to the house. I rotated around to watch him, and I saw him pause when he reached the porch steps. He went up them and then pivoted to look at me. "Was the wood like this before?"

I started walking toward him. "No. That's changed too."

This time, I went up the other side where the wood still looked worn. I would see if there was any difference by tomorrow.

I stopped dead in my tracks as I realized what I was doing. I was making plans for tomorrow like I lived here. Even worse was how casual that thought had been. How could I have lost the urgency to get home and remember who I was?

"What's wrong?" Devon asked.

Urgent words spilled out of me. "We have to get out of here."

He was immediately on alert, his gaze darting around for danger. "What's happening? Do you sense something?"

"You've lost it too," I accused. "Did you forget about the monsters? We're supposed to be trying to get home. Not looking at grass and wood. Who cares if it grew or changed color? That won't help us. We need to leave!"

"We already tried that," he reminded me in a frustrated tone.

I fixed a fierce look on him. "*You* didn't. But you're going to. I mean it, Devon. I want you to go back."

Putting up a hand to stop him before he could argue, I continued. "I'm going to try again too, but you can't just pretend. What if there's another spell in your book that could help me? It's back at your house, right?" He didn't know that Abby had brought it here, and he didn't need to.

His expression was troubled now. "But what if I can't get back to you right away? You'll be here alone."

I shoved down my fear at that thought and put on a brave face. "The protection spells worked, so I'll be fine inside the house."

Straightening my spine, I marched to the door but then braced my hand against it as I lifted my foot to pull off my muddy sock. Dropping it on the porch, I put down my bare foot and lifted the other one to remove that dirty sock too. A part of me recognized that I was still putting importance on this place, but there was no reason to track mud inside. That was the downside to the rain. It had made the dry ground muddy.

Devon followed my lead by removing his dirty shoes and trailing after me into the house. I went straight to the living room and plopped down on the floor. He sat down beside me as I stared at the book on the coffee table. It had been left open to the spell we had tried before breakfast. I fervently hoped that Devon was right, and that all I had needed was some food to replenish my strength.

I glanced over at him as I took hold of his hand. "Really do it this time. Don't pretend."

He expelled a breath before promising in a solemn tone, "I will."

"Okay," I said with determination. "Let's do this."

I turned back to the book and focused on picturing myself in the hospital.

"Squeeze my hand when you're ready," Devon said.

A quick glance at him revealed that he was looking at me. "Okay, but you focus too."

He nodded, and I turned back to concentrate on where I wanted to go. When I felt laser focused, I squeezed his hand, and we recited the spell aloud together.

This time, I felt his grip slacken, and I was sure that he was about to disappear the same way he had appeared. I held still so I wouldn't distract him, and I tried really hard to wish myself away from here too.

"I knew it!"

I jumped at the sudden sound of Devon's voice raised in anger. My head whipped toward him as he snatched his hand from my loose grip and shot up to his feet.

He looked down at me with a furious expression. "That asshole stole my body. And he's fucking *walking*. My dad is…"

A pained look came over his face, and he spun away to quickly go back outside. I wasn't sure if I should go after him or give him his space. He clearly didn't want me to see his emotional pain, but I wanted to be there for him and offer my support. Maybe talking to me about it would help.

I also wanted to know what had happened, and how he had seen Lucius walking around in his body. I hadn't even been able to get a glimpse of mine.

I went to the door and watched him through the screen. He stood at the top of the porch steps with his back to me, looking out at the rain. It began to taper off and then stopped altogether.

Slowly opening the screen door, I made my way over to him with hesitant steps. He didn't acknowledge my presence as I stood beside him, and I looked out into the distance rather than at him. He was giving off definite don't-talk-to-me vibes, so I said nothing. I hoped that my silent support would be enough for now.

The awkwardness made me aware of how uncomfortable I was in my wet clothes, even as I appreciated the fresh, earthy smell of the air after the rain. It made me wonder what I smelled like, since I'd been wearing these clothes for two days. While I'd had a shower at the castle, I'd put on the same underwear afterwards. Devon was wearing clean clothes, and I wasn't. He probably thought I was gross.

And that was exactly how I felt. "I need to take a shower," I blurted and immediately cringed. Because why would he care? He had much more important things on his mind.

"That's a good idea," he said, confirming my fears about my state of grossness. "We should get everything done before dark. You go first, and I'll keep watch. Then I'll take my shower while you keep watch."

That brought me back to the predicament we were in. How could I be worried about hygiene when darkness would bring literal monsters?

CHAPTER 10

The need to get clean didn't go away. Maybe it was a way to distract myself from my dread, but I enjoyed looking through the clothes I found in the bedroom closet. All of them were dresses from a bygone era, although not as far back in time as the ones at the castle. Just like the clothes Devon had found, these looked like they could be from the 1940's. Some were simple, and others were more stylish, but all of them made me want to play dress up.

Since I didn't have time for that, I chose a blue dress with tiny white polka dots. To my relief, there were underwear in the dresser drawers. The bras were ridiculously pointy, and the panties were basically satiny briefs for women, but they were better than wearing the same underwear day after day.

I removed the knives from the bathtub and stripped down to take my shower. There was a bar of soap and a bottle of shampoo, but no conditioner. I washed my hair anyway and reveled in the warm water after being chilled in my wet clothes. I made sure not to take too long though, since I knew that Devon also wanted to take a shower.

Drying off with the white towels, I remembered how the one at the castle had changed color. Shaking off that image, I brushed the tangles out of my brown hair with the hairbrush I had found on top of the dresser. Examining my bare face, I considered putting on the lipstick that had been beside the brush. But that would look too obvious under the circumstances, so I settled for spritzing on some perfume and brushing my teeth. Despite the toothpaste being vintage, it squeezed out like it was brand new. There were also two unopened toothbrushes still in their packages—and they were definitely modern. One was blue, and the other one was purple. I puzzled over them for a few seconds, but then I grabbed the purple one and ripped open the package.

Brushing my teeth was the final thing I needed to feel totally clean. The finishing touch was putting on fresh clothes. The dress fit me like it was made for me, and it was a flattering style with its belted waist and relaxed skirt that fell below my knees. Instead of socks, I was wearing knee high nylon stockings.

I went downstairs feeling like I had just gotten ready for a date. Devon's reaction when he saw me reinforced that impression. He was still out on the porch, and he turned at the sound of the screen door opening. His dark eyes took me in appreciatively, like a guy who was pleased with what he saw when he arrived to pick up his date.

He even spoke the words. "You look lovely."

The warm happiness blossoming in my chest bloomed into a smile on my face. "Thank you. You look..."

My eyes swept over him, and heat rose to my cheeks. His wet shirt clung to him, and the white fabric was mostly transparent. Not to mention that he'd already left the top several buttons undone, so a bit of his chest had been showing. With the weight of the wet material pulling it down, even more skin was exposed.

I'd been searching for a masculine description of lovely, but he looked *hot*.

He swiped back the dark hair plastered to his forehead, which was also hot. "I know. I look like a drowned rat. I'll go take a quick shower and put on some dry clothes."

He was sexy enough in wet clothes. I didn't need to think about him wet and naked. My face was burning now.

To my mortification, he noticed. "Your face is all red. You're not getting sick, are you?" Stepping closer, he reached out and felt my forehead with the back of his hand.

Scrambling back away from his touch, I said, "I'm fine."

He frowned. "I think you might have a fever. Maybe standing out in the rain wasn't such a good idea."

"I'm okay. Please go get dressed," I pleaded in desperation.

He looked down at himself and then back at me as comprehension dawned on his face. "You're blushing." Amusement lit up his eyes. "You probably don't remember this, but guys can go out in public without a shirt. Even your virgin eyes must have seen them."

If I had been flustered before, it was even worse now. "My what? How would you know...why would you think that?" I sputtered.

He smiled, but it was a rueful smile. "It came up in conversation."

I got the sense that he had done something he wasn't proud of, but I was more concerned with him knowing something so personal about me—something that I hadn't even known myself. If it was even true. I had no way of knowing if he actually knew this, or if he was just messing with me.

The return of his smirk proved that. "I noticed your wet shirt too," he said before walking past me and into the house.

What saved me from total humiliation was remembering that the t-shirt I had been wearing wasn't white. It was red, which was a dark enough color not to show much when it got wet. It had been clinging to me, but at least it hadn't turned transparent like Devon's shirt.

Well, I didn't feel bad for ogling him, because he had admitted to doing the same to me. Then I realized what that meant.

He was attracted to me. And he'd said it because he wanted me to know.

A sense of déjà vu came over me, like this had happened before. Getting excited, I eagerly searched my mind for the memory. And it was there. I knew it was there, and I could almost grasp it. But no matter how hard I tried, it refused to take form.

Tears of frustration welled up in my eyes. I'd finally had a spark of memory, but I couldn't access it. This was worse than remembering nothing. It was maddening to almost recall something.

I even had an idea what it was about. Devon had revealed his attraction to me before. But how? Under what circumstances? Had he flirted with me at school? He'd said that we went to school together. But were we just classmates?

I realized that we had to be more than that for him to come here looking for me. It was so obvious that it was astounding I hadn't thought about it until now. But so much had happened so fast that I hadn't had time to slow down and think things through.

Like who I was to Devon. His words from earlier came back to me. He'd said that I'd thrown myself in front of him to save his life. I couldn't imagine myself doing that. I wasn't brave or heroic. I'd done nothing but cower in fear when confronted with scary things. So, what had compelled me to put myself in danger for Devon?

Had I been in love with him? I certainly felt drawn to him, but it troubled me that I wouldn't remember such intense feelings for him. Intense enough to throw myself in front of him. I recalled that he had done the same for me when he thought that Lucius was going to hurt me.

Was Devon my boyfriend? That thought sent the butterflies in my stomach flurrying in excitement.

But if he was, why hadn't he told me that? And why hadn't he wanted to kiss me? Maybe he was mad that I didn't remember him.

Or maybe we were just friends. But then why wouldn't he have said that? Abby had told me right away that she was my friend. Devon had only told me his name, and that we went to school together.

It was so frustrating not being able to remember! Relying on other people to tell me sucked. I couldn't be sure if what they told me was true. Even if it was, they could be holding things back and not telling me the whole story. That was what I suspected Devon was doing. He claimed it was because he didn't want to influence me into creating false memories, but maybe he had a different reason.

What had happened between us in the past that he didn't want to tell me about? I focused again, but this time I pictured Devon and just let my mind drift. Yet no memory surfaced except for the recent ones with him. Nothing from the past.

But I'd had that momentary flash of familiarity earlier, so he was the key to remembering. I needed more of those moments with him. A plan began to form in my mind about how to make that happen. One thing that I'd learned was that casual was the best approach with Devon. He closed up when things got too intense. I needed to keep it light, or at least neutral. Considering the situation we were in, that wasn't going to be the easiest task. But I vowed to keep my emotions under control.

There was also the problem of how we were going to get back to our bodies. That was such a weird concept that was still hard for me to grasp. I felt real and solid right here. I still needed food and water. I could touch objects and move them. I could get soaked by the rain. There was nothing ghostly or spirit-like about me. I even had to go to the bathroom like a real person. I had a physical body right here, so how could I have another one somewhere else?

That's when it struck me what might be preventing me from returning to that body. Was my own uncertainty holding me back? If it was, how could I overcome it?

As I pondered that, it occurred to me that I could use this to get Devon to tell me more about myself. He would have to help me if it was the only way for me to get back. Which brought me to the problem of how he could get his body back. There had to be a way.

I went back inside and picked up the spell book. Thinking it over, the only thing I could come up with was that this was a case of possession. That made it sound so creepy, and I supposed that it must have been for Devon when he saw that someone else had taken over his body and was living his life.

Flipping back to the beginning, I went through the entire book again in search of a spell that could help him. But there was nothing involving possession or switching bodies. Maybe this wasn't the only book of spells though. Setting it down on the coffee table, I moved to the stairs and started up them. I halted when I saw Devon, who was at the top of the staircase, and who had apparently been about to come downstairs.

He was freshly showered, his hair damp but no longer sopping wet. He'd put on dry clothes that made him look like the old-fashioned suitor I'd pictured taking me on a date when I'd put on this vintage dress. Yet he wasn't a gentleman in a faded photograph from the past. He was a living, flesh and blood man who'd left the top few buttons of his shirt carelessly open again. That tantalizing glimpse of skin was superimposed over the image in my mind of him in that wet, transparent shirt.

My eyes lifted to his face and met his gaze. We stood entranced, the magic between us undeniable. I had all the butterflies and tingles. Time stopped, and something stirred at the back of my mind. Real and vivid.

It went beyond déjà vu. A true memory of this exact thing happening. Devon's dark eyes and a pivotal moment in my life that had the enchantment of a fairytale.

Love at first sight? Was that what I was remembering? I had a vague recollection of a hallway, and possibly there had been other people there. School? That felt right, but I wasn't entirely sure. All I remembered clearly was Devon's face and eyes, but this Devon before me was superimposed over the one from my memory, so I couldn't make out all the details.

"I remember!" I exclaimed, filled with excitement and wanting to share it with him.

My voice broke the trance he was in along with the magical mood. His demeanor changed from spellbound to guarded as he asked, "You do?"

"Yeah," I answered, disappointment in his reaction bringing down my enthusiasm. "It was about you. I think I..."

How could I tell him that I thought I'd fallen in love with him at first sight? "I think, uh, that we were at school."

He looked at me expectantly, waiting for more.

"We were, uh, in the hallway, and there were other people in the background."

His expression turned deadpan as he watched me. "That's it?"

"Well, it's something," I said, hearing the defensiveness in my voice. "I finally remembered something."

"And what an important memory."

"It's important to me," I shot back. "You don't know what it's like not to remember anything."

In my agitation, I started walking up the stairs toward him. "I think it's why I haven't been able to go home. Because I don't remember this other me. I don't know this other life, so how can I go back to it?"

My words struck him, and I saw realization dawning on his face. "I think you're right."

Lost in thought, he absently stepped back at my approach and let me past him. When I stepped into the hallway, I went around to the third-floor stairway instead of continuing on to the second-floor bedrooms.

Devon followed me. "Where are you going?"

"I want to see if there's another spell book."

My time up here had been interrupted by the arrival of Lucius, so I hadn't explored it as much as I'd wanted to. The turret bedroom charmed me anew. Light spilled in through the tall windows set in the circular wall, and it was brighter than the last time I'd been in here. Moving closer, I saw that some of the clouds had cleared after the rain to let a bit of the sunshine through. It lifted my spirits, but I still scanned the tree line for any sign of encroaching darkness. When there was none, I turned my attention to the curved window seat beneath the windows. Drawers were set into it below the seat cushion, making it a storage area as well.

I crouched down and began to open them. There were letters that I had to resist reading as I reminded myself of my mission. I was searching for a book, not the loose photographs I found in other drawers. I would look at those later if I had time. Finally, I came across a leather-bound diary and snatched it up. While it wasn't a spell book, I thought it might be useful—at least in finding out some information about who lived here. Setting it on the window seat, I rose and turned to confront Devon, who was rifling through the dresser drawers.

"Do you have to slam them shut? You're going to break them."

"Who cares?" he threw back. "It's not like we're going to be able to sell them. There's no one here to buy them."

"We also can't buy anymore," I pointed out. "So, we need to take care of what we have."

He whirled on me. "That's your solution? We're going to give up and stay here?"

"No," I denied, but a part of me was hurt. It had seemed like he liked me. While our situation wasn't ideal, we were here together. I'd thought he'd at least appreciate that much and see it as the bright side of our ordeal.

"I'm looking for a way for you to get your body back," I reminded him.

"That's not going to happen! He's not leaving it now that he has it."

"Then you'll have to kick him out."

He snorted and settled back into sarcasm. "Of course. Why didn't I think of that?"

"He's taken over your body, so we need a spell against possession."

"An exorcism. This just gets better and better."

My irritation flared at his attitude. "I'm trying to help you. The least you could do is work with me instead of making snide comments."

He saluted me. "I'll get right on that. It shouldn't take long to find a priest."

I rolled my eyes. "We don't need a priest. He's not a demon."

His expression darkened. "He might be easier to get rid of if he was."

CHAPTER 11

"Why would anyone take someone else's body? And where's his body?" I asked.

"He doesn't have one," Devon answered flatly.

"What? How could he not have one? He's not a ghost."

Devon sighed a long-suffering sigh. "I don't want to get into this again. He wants my life, and that's all you need to know."

Frustration exploded out of me. "It is not! Stop keeping things from me. I need to know everything if I'm going to help you get him out."

His expression turned grim. "You almost got killed the last time you went up against him. You better stay out of it."

"But he didn't hurt me when he took me to his castle," I pointed out.

"That's because you weren't a threat to him. But as soon as you are, he'll kill you."

"No, he won't," I insisted. "He's not a killer. Nobody who plays music with so much emotion can be evil. Whatever he did had to be some kind of accident. Or maybe it was a prank that went too far. Just some kind of misunderstanding."

"I was there, Hazel! I saw him do it, and it was no fucking misunderstanding. He tried to murder me." He spun away and stalked out of the room and down the stairs.

I took off after him, following on his heels and demanding the full story. "How did he try to murder you? What did he do?"

He kept going without saying a word as he marched down the second-floor hallway.

"Tell me!"

My fury grew as he ignored me and quickly descended the stairs to the first floor, with me right behind him. "Are you lying? Is that why you can't tell me what happened? Because nothing did. You're making it all up!"

He halted and turned, his dark eyes blazing with anger.

And the house began to shake.

I gasped in fear and stared at him in horror, convinced that he was doing this. But his eyes widened in surprise. "Earthquake! Run!"

He grabbed my hand, and we sprinted toward the door. Yanking it open, he let go and ushered me out ahead of him. We ran across the porch and down the steps.

"Get away from the house," he yelled.

Heart pounding, I raced into the grass and stumbled to a stop a good distance away. The earth shook beneath my feet as I turned to see if the house was still standing. To my immense relief, the shaking ended without taking it down. We would have nowhere to hide from the monsters without it. I glanced back at the trees to make sure the darkness wasn't creeping up on us.

"I hope there's no damage," Devon said.

"It looks okay to me," I told him and started walking back.

"Wait. There might be an aftershock. We should give it a few minutes to be sure it's over."

I threw another glance over my shoulder. "Let's get closer to the house, just in case."

He pulled his phone out of his pocket as he walked beside me. "Fucking great. The battery is dead, and I don't have a charger. I don't know what time it is anymore."

"I wonder why there aren't any clocks here."

"Because we're in some weird other dimension. This is close enough," he said and halted about twenty feet away from the house.

I stopped too and turned to look at him. "We're in another dimension?"

"How else do you explain the way it gets dark here? The sun sets everywhere on earth. It doesn't just get blotted out from the sky. And where does the darkness come from if not from the sun setting? None of it makes any sense."

"And there are monsters," I added with another uneasy glance back at the tree-line. "Maybe we should go inside now."

"Wait out here. I'll go in and check for damage."

"No," I protested. "I'll go with you."

He gave me an impatient look. "Hazel, please, just let me do this. I'll be back in a minute to let you know if it's safe."

"Why? Because you're the guy and you have to protect me? I can take care of myself," I insisted, although I liked that he cared about my safety.

"I know you can, but what if something happens to me? How are you going to help me if you get hurt too?"

I narrowed my eyes at him, knowing that he was using a tactic to get his way. I could have argued that I should be the one to go inside instead of him, but I didn't want to waste any more time. The darkness could start creeping toward us soon.

"Okay, but be careful. And hurry. I'll keep watch out here."

"Good plan," he said as if I had come up with it.

I pursed my lips but gave in to a reluctant smile. He smiled back, and the butterflies in my belly stirred to life.

His smile warmed and lightened his tone. "I'll be right back."

I watched him dart up the porch steps and into the house, and I felt like everything would be okay. We would figure everything out together and find our way back home. When we were out of mortal danger, we'd be free to explore our attraction to each other. My mind drifted off into fantasies of holding hands as we walked down the hall together at school and kissing him goodnight after a date.

A sudden sense of being watched abruptly halted my daydreaming. Alarm shot through my bloodstream as I remembered that I was supposed to be keeping an eye on the tree-line. Was that what I was feeling? Were the monsters right behind me? I was afraid to look, but I had to. So, I did it fast, spinning around to face what I hoped was just my imagination.

Horror stole my breath when I saw the darkness creeping past the trees and over the grass on its way toward me. Frozen in terror, I couldn't get my voice to work or my feet to move.

Someone grabbed me, and I thought it was Devon at first. It wasn't until he lifted me onto a horse that I realized it was Lucius. He was seated behind me, and we were galloping away before I could even think of struggling. Just like last time, fear kept me docile because we were racing away from the darkness.

"Devon doesn't know it's coming," I said, finally finding my voice.

"Why would he leave you outside alone? What kind of protector is he?"

I didn't have time to argue with him about not needing protection. "He went inside to check for damage after the earthquake, and I was supposed to keep watch, but I wasn't paying attention. I didn't warn him! He doesn't know."

"There was an earthquake? Are you sure?"

"Of course, I'm sure! The house was shaking, and we ran outside, and the ground was shaking."

"That's odd. There's never been an earthquake here before."

"Who cares? Devon is in danger! If he goes outside and the monsters get him again, it will be my fault."

"They got him? And he survived. Damn, how disappointing."

"That's not funny. He was really hurt. I don't know if he would have made it if I hadn't done the healing spell."

"And how did you know how to do that? You've claimed to be ignorant of magic, but it seems you were lying. Have you also faked your amnesia?"

"I didn't fake anything," I insisted indignantly. "I found a spell book in the house, and there was a healing spell in it."

"Since you conjured the house, you conjured the spell book as well. Which means that you knew those spells or brought them here with you."

I opened my mouth to argue but got distracted by a beam of sunlight that shone down on us and warmed my skin. We were out of it too quickly, but it awakened hope in me that we would all be okay.

"What the hell?"

"What?" I asked, instantly alarmed by his dismay.

"The sunshine," he said. "There's never any sunshine here."

"Of course there is," I contradicted and pointed up at the sky. "There's the sun."

"But it's never that bright. In your world, you can't look directly at the sun. But you can here, and you never feel its warmth. Even when it's not hidden behind clouds."

"Well, you're wrong, because I just felt it on my skin."

"I did too, but I never have before."

"Maybe because you live in the fog," I suggested. "You should have picked a better place to build your castle."

"You don't understand. I've wandered this entire world and never felt the sun's warmth. This has never happened before."

I found that hard to believe but let it go. "Well, it's all new to me. Just like the rain today. I can't decide which one I like better. The rain is fun, and it makes everything smell fresh and earthy. But the sun lifts your spirits—and protects you from monsters. So, the sun wins, now that I think about it."

"It rained?" he asked like it was something shocking.

"Yeah," I replied, wondering why that was so surprising. "I stood outside in it and got soaked, but it was worth it."

"It never rains here," he said.

I craned my head back to look at him and caught a horrifying sight behind him. "It's gaining on us! Go faster!"

I faced forward again and willed the horse to outrun the darkness that I knew would soon overtake us. My heart hammered in fear, and I held on tight to the saddle.

"It's okay, Hazel," he soothed. "They can't hurt you when you're with me."

Diablo neighed, and it set my nerves even more on edge. Then I was within the darkness, and I saw it creeping past me. I stared at it in wide-eyed terror as I tried to remember the protection spell.

"Calm down. You're safe with me."

My lungs seized at the sound of the demonic voice behind me. Ice cold dread kept me frozen for long seconds until the unknown horror became unbearable. I had to see what was behind me. And I was met with a sight that stopped my heart.

Red, glowing eyes stared back at me. It had Lucius's face, but it was evil. It was going to kill me!

That's when the veil lifted, and I remembered everything.

He *had* almost killed me. He'd tricked me into helping him and combined our power against Devon. My dreams had warned me that Lucius was malevolent, but this went way beyond creepy Devon. This was a demon.

I flailed in panic, trying to escape him. He tightened his grip, and I looked down as I tried to wrench his hands from around my middle, only to see that he now had claws instead of fingernails.

"Hazel, no," he said in that warped voice straight from some satanic possession movie. "You'll fall off."

I fought harder as I screamed in terror. The horse screeched and bucked, jolting me as we came to a sudden stop. Lucius pulled me down before I realized that he had already dismounted. I stumbled as he let me go, and I backed slowly away from him.

"Get a hold of yourself. You can't ride in hysterics. Take Diablo and get to safety. He knows the way."

The demonic voice came out of his mouth as he watched me with those unearthly red eyes. As I took another step back, I caught sight of Diablo, and a fresh wave of terror swept over me. He was now a demon horse straight from hell with ears that looked like horns and unnatural glowing red eyes that stood out from his black face. He bared his teeth with an unholy shriek, showing sharp canines protruding from both the top and bottom of his jaw.

"They're here," his master said and whirled to face the monsters I had somehow forgotten about.

He slashed at them with his claws as Diablo joined him and stomped on them with his fiery hooves, which also scorched them with flames.

I turned and ran for my life.

CHAPTER 12

I screamed as I fell into a dark void.

"Oh my God, she's awake! Hazel, it's okay, we're here."

I blinked open my eyes at the sound of my mom's voice and squeezed them shut again immediately against the fluorescent brightness in the room.

A room! And my mom! I wasn't in the nightmare world with demons and monsters anymore. Squinting to let my eyes adjust, I peeked at my mom's beloved face. Relief washed over me. I knew her, and I knew—everything. I remembered my entire life.

"Mom." I wanted to say more, but I didn't know where to start.

"I'm here," she said, smiling through her tears as she took my hand. "You're going to be okay."

My dad burst into the room, followed by a nurse. He rushed over to me but spoke to my mom. "How is she?"

"Good," I answered, so he'd know that I could talk. "I had amnesia, but now I remember everything."

"Was she disoriented when she regained consciousness?" the nurse asked.

"No," Mom replied. "She was screaming when she came to, like she was waking up from a nightmare. But she knew me as soon as she opened her eyes."

"That's a good sign," the nurse said. "I'll check her vitals, and the doctor will be in shortly."

As Mom moved aside for her, I realized that I couldn't tell the hospital staff about being in another dimension. They'd think I was crazy, and I'd be stuck in here as they ran all kinds of tests on my brain and did mental evaluations on me.

It did all seem farfetched, but it had been so real. Mom had mentioned a nightmare, but that couldn't be what it was. Could it? I didn't tell the nurse, but I did feel disoriented and confused. It was weird to wake up in the hospital seconds after being somewhere else. And how had I gotten here? I hadn't even done the spell to get back. I'd just spontaneously been transported.

The more I thought about it, the more I doubted that any of it had happened. A world where magic and monsters were real? It was far more likely that it had been a vivid dream brought on by my coma.

I asked the doctor if it was possible to dream while in a coma, and he said that some patients have reported having dreams. Of course, that led him to ask me if I'd dreamt anything. I lied and said that I thought I'd had a nightmare but couldn't remember it.

He asked me questions about what I had been doing on the night I lost consciousness and why I was on the floor. Since I couldn't tell him that I had been trying to contact a guy I'd talked to telepathically, I made up a story about doing meditation. After examining me, he pronounced me healthy and said that I should be able to go home in the morning.

"But what caused her coma?" my dad demanded. "You haven't given us any reason for it. How did it happen?"

"There is no physical reason—no head trauma, drugs, stroke, or any other medical conditions. I've done a little research, and in rare cases, coma can be the result of excessive, ongoing stress. It's called a psychogenic coma. If you're interested, I can recommend a mental health professional."

"Yes, we are," Dad said to my disappointment. "We want to prevent this from happening again."

"What have you been stressed out about?" Mom asked me.

Her expression immediately transformed from concerned to remorseful. "Everything that happened with Matt, and then Abby! Of course you're overwhelmed. You've gone through so much in such a short time. I should have realized that you needed help to deal with it."

"Mom, I'm okay. Really, I am."

She patted my arm. "Everything will be fine. Get some rest. I'll be right here if you need me."

"Rest?" I exclaimed. "I just woke up after...how long has it been?"

"Three days," Dad said, his haggard face showing the toll of those days. "You gave us quite a scare."

"I've been lazing around for all that time," I quipped, trying to lighten the mood. "I don't need any more rest."

Only the doctor smiled at my attempt at humor. "It's great that you feel well-rested, but you should still try to get some sleep tonight."

"Can't I go home now? You said yourself that there's nothing wrong with me."

"I'd like to keep you here overnight for observation. You only just regained consciousness, so it's better not to rush it."

My parents agreed with him, so I had to stay there until morning. I didn't mind much though, because it was great to be in a world without monsters. What was a night in the hospital compared to being trapped in the dark with nightmare creatures and red-eyed demons?

I shivered at the memory, and I was glad that my mom had decided to stay with me despite my insistence that she should go home and get some sleep. Her dark circles looked even worse than the ones under my dad's eyes. She had sent him home with a brief but loving goodnight kiss that conveyed the love they shared. It was a familiar sight, but I was seeing it with new eyes. They liked each other. The warmth and caring they had for each other was something I'd always taken for granted before. But being away from them for days, and even forgetting that they existed, was making me notice things I usually didn't pay attention to. Like how wonderful my parents' love was.

It made me happy and hopeful that I could have that with someone someday. My thoughts strayed to Devon. That was the one part of my dream I wished could have been real—the time I'd gotten to spend with him. Too bad we hadn't kissed. I would have loved to have experienced that again, even if it was only in my dreams.

"You should text Abby and tell her that you're okay," Mom said. "She's been so worried about you."

She held my phone out to me. "Tell her that you'll talk to her tomorrow when you get home. I don't want you calling her now and getting overly emotional. I'm still hoping you'll get some sleep tonight."

I eagerly took it from her. "Thanks! It sucked having no phones."

She gave me a strange look but didn't say anything. I realized that I'd just complained about having no phones in a coma. "In my dream," I explained. "There were no phones in my dream."

"So, you remember it? Why were you screaming? What happened?"

I decided that it didn't matter if I told her, since it was only a dream. "I was in this weird place, and I had amnesia. And there were these monsters that came out at night."

"How terrifying," Mom said, her eyes filled with sympathy. "You were trapped in a nightmare you couldn't wake up from. It was so scary not being able to bring you back to consciousness, but you looked peaceful at least. But you were suffering too."

"It wasn't all bad," I hurried to assure her. "Devon was there, and I even got to see Abby. They told me who I was, and that I was in a coma. I tried to do a spell to get back to my body." I smiled at the silliness of it. "Of course I could do magic. I'm from Salem, after all. I'm surprised that I wasn't riding around on a broomstick."

But Mom had an amazed expression on her face. "You heard them. You didn't hear us, but you heard your friends. Both Abby and Devon came to visit you and—oh my gosh, you won't believe the news about Devon! It's a miracle!"

My stomach dropped, and dread took hold of me. "What?" I asked, fearing the answer.

She beamed at me. "He can walk!"

CHAPTER 13

My stunned expression got me through that revelation, which was supposed to be a miraculous, wonderful one that should have made me ecstatically happy. Instead, as Mom went on about this miracle, I was grappling with the horrible suspicion that my dream had been real.

Then I had the idea that maybe Devon had told me that he could walk while I'd been in a coma, and it had gotten tangled up in my dream. Mom had said that he'd been here visiting me. I hoped that was it, but I needed to talk to Abby to know for sure.

Luckily, she saw my text right away and responded to it.

> Finally! What took you so long? I was worried you'd be stuck there forever

> It was real?

> Castle, room of stars, Lucius, magic spell? Yep

> Thought it was a dream! Wish my mom would let me call you. Making me go to sleep

I set my phone on the little table beside my bed and said goodnight to my mom. She turned off the lights, leaving just the illumination spilling in from the hallway. After telling me to let her know if I needed anything, she sat down in the recliner and put her feet up. I closed my eyes for a minute, and she was asleep when I opened them. She was clearly exhausted and needed the rest.

I didn't, but I stayed put in the hospital bed. I was reeling from finding out that I had been in another world. And Devon was still there! How was he going to get out when Lucius had stolen his body? Mom had confirmed it when she told me that he could walk. That was exactly what Devon had said he'd seen when he'd tried to return to his body. Lucius had been walking around in it as he took over his life.

Which meant that he was the one who'd visited me while I was unconscious—not Devon. A chill ran down my spine as an image of his demon red eyes flashed through my mind. And he had a demon horse. No wonder he'd named it Diablo.

But wait! He'd been back in the other world to kidnap me. In order to do that, he'd had to leave Devon's body. Devon could get back into it! But did he know? Had he tried? Maybe he was already back like I was.

I grabbed my phone and quickly texted him.

There was no response, and my heart sank. As the time stretched into long minutes, I told myself that he could be asleep. It was getting late, and his body hadn't gotten as much rest as mine. But I couldn't shake the worry.

What if he was still over there? What if the monsters had hurt him again and he needed my help? What if demon Lucius had come after him after I escaped?

My heart seized at that thought, and I wanted to go to him immediately. But what if he was here and I went back there for nothing? What if I got trapped there—this time by myself. I couldn't risk it until I knew for sure where he was.

Glancing over at my mom, I knew that I couldn't do that to her and my dad. Leaving my body would put me back into a coma. I couldn't put them through that again. Last time, it had happened spontaneously without my knowledge. The force of being hit with Lucius's power must have knocked me unconscious. But it hadn't just been his power. He'd tricked me into combining mine with his, and he'd tried to use it against Devon. To kill Devon.

But had he really planned to kill him? Or had he wanted to knock him unconscious so he could send him to that other world and steal his body? The blast meant for Devon hadn't killed me. Was that because it wasn't meant to, or because he'd held back at the last second when he'd seen me jump in front of Devon?

Now that I remembered everything, I recalled the dream I'd had about Lucius and his demon horse. Had that been a premonition? I'd never had premonitions before, but I'd also never known that I had magical powers. Even Lucius had been surprised by my ability to bring color to his world.

Which brought me back to whether he was good or bad. He'd treated me like a guest in his castle, but he was terrifying in his demon form. My mind paused on that thought. How could he have a demon form? He was either a demon or he wasn't. Devon had said that he wasn't. But people didn't transform into beings with glowing red eyes and claws where their fingernails used to be.

The closest thing to what I'd seen were vampire movies in which they looked like normal people until they showed their vampire faces. But Lucius didn't have fangs, so I didn't think he was a vampire. He'd had his same gorgeous face apart from the demonic red eyes. The term handsome devil popped into my head, and it creeped me out in this context. I hadn't been far off in thinking of him as creepy Devon.

Yet now that I was away from him and could think clearly, I remembered the last thing I'd seen him doing before I had jumped back into my body. He'd been slashing at the monsters with his wicked claws. He could have torn me to shreds with them, but he'd been fighting the monsters instead.

Was he evil or not? Maybe he'd had some other horrible plan for me.

Maybe he had become possessed since I'd last seen him. Because he hadn't looked like a demon at night when we'd been in his castle. What had happened to him after I left? Was it the spell he'd used to steal Devon's body? Had he somehow summoned a demon while casting it, and it had taken possession of him?

My skin crawled at the thought. We might need a priest to do an exorcism after all.

Time crept by slowly as I anxiously waited for morning. I drifted off at some point and awoke to the sound of my mom talking with a nurse. Relieved to finally see daylight, I sat up, ready and eager to leave.

Mom rushed over to my side and adjusted my pillow so I could lean back against it. "How are you feeling?"

"Great. Do you have my clothes? I need to get dressed."

"Let me check your vitals, and then you can have your breakfast," the nurse said.

Mom stepped back out of the way so I could be assessed. I answered questions about my pain level, which was zero. There was nothing wrong with me, but I still had to wait for the doctor to see me and declare me well enough to go home. So, I ate the toast and scrambled eggs to make everyone happy.

The waffles I'd had with Devon had tasted much better. Hospital food couldn't compete with magic waffles. A hospital room also couldn't compete with an enchanting old house, complete with turret rooms I'd barely gotten to explore. I felt a weird nostalgia for the place and wished that I'd taken advantage of the time I'd had there. My childhood self would have loved to rummage around in a house like that. But I'd been concerned with my amnesia and everything else that was happening.

Like the fact that I was there with Devon. Too bad I hadn't known who he was, and that I'd had a crush on him for years—and that he'd kissed me.

But maybe it was better that I hadn't known all that, because it would have made things awkward. I thought back to those magical moments in the rain and knew that I wouldn't have felt as free to delight in it in front of him. I remembered his warm smile and knew that he wouldn't have responded in the same way if I'd known him. Because we hadn't left off on good terms.

He'd rejected me after those hot, passionate kisses we'd shared. Then I'd basically teamed up with his enemy against him and almost gotten him killed. Yet I'd thrown myself in front of him, which had probably redeemed me and shown him how much I cared about him.

He'd shown that he cared about me too by taking the risk of coming to find me. My heartbeat picked up speed as I thought about that. While Abby had done the same thing, she'd been my best friend since elementary school. Devon had declared that our intense connection was physical, and nothing more. But he'd put himself in danger for me. That told me that I meant more to him than he'd said.

I really needed to know if he was okay. I checked my phone for a text from him, but there was still nothing. My anxiety spiked, but I had to act like everything was okay. Mom might have believed that I had talked to a ghost as a child, but telling her that I was afraid a demon had possessed Devon's body would make her question my sanity. On the off chance that she did believe me, she would try to protect me by keeping me away from him. I couldn't risk that, because I had to help Devon.

But she picked up on something with her mother's intuition. "What's wrong?"

I thought fast. "I was just thinking about how many days of school I've missed and how much homework I have to catch up on."

She waved that away. "They'll give you plenty of time. You were in a coma for goodness' sake! I'll call and make sure they accommodate you, because the last thing you need is more stress."

I groaned as I remembered the doctor's theory that my coma had been caused by excessive stress—and that I would have to see a therapist. "I'm fine, Mom. I can handle some extra homework. I was just complaining to complain. That means I'm back to normal, right?" I teased.

Mom smiled in response, but her concerned eyes showed that she wasn't at the joking stage yet. I had to remember that from her perspective, I'd been in a comatose state for days. She didn't know that I'd been conscious somewhere else and doing okay for the most part.

Now that I thought about it, I'd handled everything pretty well for my first time being on my own without my parents. I'd done the smart thing by searching for shelter and help from the police. I'd had enough sense to be wary of Lucius, despite his beautiful face. I'd taken charge and helped Devon when he was injured. And I'd done it all while I had amnesia.

How much better would I do now that I had my memory back? My confidence soared, and I was sure that I could defeat Lucius and help Devon get his body back. If he wasn't in it already. Maybe he'd spontaneously gone back to his body just like I had.

My mood lifted even more when I was allowed to put on my own clothes after the doctor said I could go home. I momentarily paused as I looked at the socks, which I remembered leaving in Lucius's castle. They had been dirty from me walking around outside in them. But they were still clean here. I knew they were the same pair, because they had little red hearts at the ankle.

"I have shoes for you," Mom said, misunderstanding why I was staring at my socks. "You weren't wearing any when they brought you in, but I brought some for you the next day." She pulled a plastic bag out of the cabinet and removed a pair of sneakers, setting them down on the floor beside the bed.

"Thanks. Could you pull the curtain?"

She did, and I got dressed in private. I was glad to get out of the hospital gown and into real clothes. It was the final thing I had needed to feel like myself again. Opening the curtain, I strode over to my mom and gave her a hug.

It was instant comfort, and I reveled in it. How could I have forgotten this? How could I have forgotten my mom? "I love you," I told her, trying to make up for forgetting her even though she didn't know I had.

I couldn't remember the last time I had said it to her, though I felt it all the time. I used to say it a lot when I was a kid, but it had somehow become childish in my mind as I got closer to becoming a teenager. That seemed ridiculous now, because there was nothing immature about telling people that you loved them.

"I love you too," she said. "So much. I'm so happy you're okay."

"Me too," I said, wondering what would have happened if I'd died in that other world. Would I have died in this one as well?

The cold chill that ran down my back was accompanied by a male voice I knew. "You're back."

CHAPTER 14

let go of my mom and turned toward him. It was Devon, and he was standing in the doorway.

"I apologize for intruding," he said. "I came to check on Hazel's condition, and I am delighted to see that she has returned."

"Yes, we got our own miracle," Mom said.

"Indeed," he replied. "It is a miraculous time for us. Everything is as it should be."

I narrowed my eyes at him, trying to figure out if he was really Devon. "Didn't you get my text? I told you I was back."

I saw the confusion in his eyes before he covered it. "I didn't get it. My apologies."

"You don't know what a text is," I accused. "Because you've never used a phone." I pointed my finger at him. "You're not him!"

Mom blocked my view of him as she got in front of me and placed her hands on my shoulders. "Hazel, honey, calm down. Everything is okay. Remember I told you that Devon can walk now? I know it must be a shock to you seeing him out of his wheelchair, but you can't get stressed out."

She looked over her shoulder at him while still keeping hold of me. "I'm so sorry. I know she's happy for you. She's just disoriented after being in a coma, and she needs some time to adjust."

"Of course," he said. "I shall leave you."

I sidestepped out of Mom's grasp and saw him turn and walk off down the hallway. He was here in our world. Lucius was here.

So where was Devon? Was he trapped back in the other world—alone? I thought about him being there all by himself with no one to help him, and I tried not to panic. A horrible thought entered my mind, but I pushed it down and repeated to myself that Devon was okay. He was okay, and I was going to fix this and get him back to his body.

I hadn't been able to get back to my body at first either, but here I was. Never mind that I didn't know how I'd done it, and that there hadn't been a demon possessing my body. Nope, I was not going to get overwhelmed and sink into despair. I hadn't given up when I'd been thrown into a world with actual monsters, and I wasn't going to do it now that I was back home on my turf. Lucius was in my world now, and he clearly didn't know everything about this place.

It was disorienting for me too, and I'd only been gone a few days. There were so many people as we left my hospital room after I got the discharge papers. Patients in every room we passed, along with family members in many of them. Nurses, doctors, and orderlies moved down the hallways as they did their jobs. We took a crowded elevator down to the main floor, and it really drove home the emptiness of Lucius's world. Here were all these people packed into this one space, and there was no one in the vast expanse of his castle or during the trek to it.

Noise bombarded me as we stepped outside the hospital doors. A constant stream of cars whizzed past on the road just beyond the parking lot, and I stared at the flow of traffic. How had I not noticed before how loud it was? And had there always been this many people? And was the sun always this bright? I put my hand up to my forehead to shield my eyes from it.

"Are you okay?" Mom asked. "Do you have a headache? Maybe I should have gotten the car and had them bring you out."

"No," I assured her. "My head's fine. I'm just not used to the sun being this bright." Because it hadn't been in the other world. There was a big difference in intensity, I now realized.

"We'll get you home, and you can rest in your room with the blinds closed."

The last thing I needed was to waste more time laying around, but I didn't argue. This excuse would come in handy when I needed to go back and get Devon. I just had to make sure that I wasn't gone long enough for her to see that I was in a coma again. I couldn't put her and my dad through that again. I would have to enlist Abby's help with that.

I'd already texted her that we were leaving the hospital, and she showed up about ten minutes after we got home. Stalling Mom from making me lay down had been easy, because I'd gone straight to the kitchen and grabbed a box of cereal off the fridge.

"That hospital breakfast wasn't good," I'd complained. "I'm craving some Cocoa Puffs."

"It was much healthier for you than that," Mom said, but she got the milk out for me along with a bowl and spoon.

My mind flashed to Devon lecturing me about healthy eating during the one and only time I'd gotten to sit with him in the cafeteria. Would I ever see him at school again? The real him, not Lucius pretending to be him. The horrible realization hit me that I'd be forced to see him there daily if we weren't able to exorcise him from Devon's body. He'd be roaming the halls with no one knowing that a demon walked among us.

And what would happen to Devon? Would he spend the rest of his life alone in that strange world? How often could I go visit him? How would I be able to live my life knowing that he was trapped there? A hollow feeling spread through my chest at the thought.

No! I wouldn't let that happen. Crunching on the chocolate cereal with determination, I prepared for battle.

I sprang up from my chair when the doorbell rang and raced to answer the door. Mom called out in alarm for me to slow down as she hurried after me, but I ignored her. Reaching my destination, I yanked open the front door and almost hit Abby with the screen door in my haste to get to her.

I threw my arms around her. "I can't believe I forgot you! I can't believe you came looking for me. Thank you so much! You're the best friend ever!"

"Yes, thank you, Abby," Mom said. "Your visits did wonders for Hazel. She apparently heard your voice while she was in a coma, and it helped bring her back. We can't thank you enough for what you've done for her."

I let go of Abby and stepped back, giving her a look that told her to play along with my mom's version of events.

"Yeah, of course. I'm so glad she's back—uh, I mean, out of her coma."

"Yeah," I said, grabbing Abby's hand and pulling her into the house. "We need to catch up."

"But you need to rest," Mom protested.

"You just said that Abby brought me back," I reminded her. "Don't you think seeing her will be better for me than taking a nap?"

Mom looked torn. "Okay, but take it easy. No more running through the house. You don't want to over exert yourself and end up back in the hospital."

I gave her a sheepish smile. "Sorry. I was just excited. I promise we'll relax and just talk."

"Good. Don't forget that Abby is still recovering too," she reminded me.

I started, because I had forgotten that. I'd been so concerned with Devon and myself that it had slipped my mind that my best friend had a life-threatening medical condition. I turned my head to stare at her. "Your heart! You shouldn't have taken a chance like that to come find me. Are you okay?"

Her expression conveyed that we needed to have this conversation in private. "I'm fine. I'm taking my medicine, and everything is good."

"Awesome," I said and started leading her up to my room.

"What about your cereal?" Mom called up the stairs. "Do you want to finish it?"

I halted and turned around to go back downstairs. "Wait, Abby. Let's go to the kitchen first."

"Okay," she said and turned to descend the stairs.

I followed her, since she was now ahead of me. Mom offered her something to eat, but she declined, saying that she'd already eaten breakfast. It was getting closer to lunchtime now, which worried me. I wanted to get back to Devon before nightfall. Grabbing my spoon and my bowl, I quickly ate the cereal that was left in it while standing instead of taking the time to sit down. Then I brought the bowl to my mouth and tipped it so I could drink the remaining milk.

Setting it back down on the table, I produced a smile for my mom.

"Thanks. We'll be in my room—relaxing. If that's okay," I added, knowing that I was taking advantage of my supposed stress-induced coma recovery, and promising myself that I would make it up to her by cleaning the house as soon as I helped Devon.

"Of course," she said. "Let me know if you need anything."

"We will," I said. "Thanks, Mom."

This time we made it up to my room without interruption, and I shut the door before urgently telling Abby about Lucius stealing Devon's body.

She gaped at me and then looked strangely relieved. "That explains it. I thought I was…"

When she failed to continue, I asked, "You thought you were what?"

Her gaze flitted to mine and then away. "Oh, um, it just felt different. I mean he was different."

"Yeah, because he's a demon. We've got to find a priest fast." I patted my pockets and glanced around. "I think I left my phone downstairs. Look up churches on yours. I don't know how I'm going to get my mom to let me leave the house, but we have to…"

I trailed off as I noticed Abby sinking down onto my bed with a shell-shocked expression. Her face had turned ashen. "Hey, are you okay? Do you need me to call an ambulance?"

Flashbacks of her collapsing lifeless on the floor had me rushing to her in panic. "Where's your phone?"

She swatted my hand away. "I'm fine. What do you mean he's a demon?"

I lifted my hand to my heart. "Geez, you scared me. I thought you were—"

"Hazel," she cut me off impatiently, "what the hell do you mean he's a demon? You said he wasn't."

"I don't have time to explain that right now. We have to save Devon first. I'm going to go talk to him real quick while you look up churches."

"What?" she exclaimed. "Are you crazy? Lucius told us never to go back there."

"I don't care what he said. Devon is stuck there, and this is the only way I can talk to him."

"What about psychically?" she suggested. "The way you talked to him before."

I considered it and shook my head. "I can't take the chance of Lucius hearing us. Then he'll know our plan. I've got to go talk to Devon in person. I need you to cover for me if my mom comes up here. Tell her I'm taking a nap."

"I don't think you should do this. What if you go into a coma again? You don't know how awful it was not being able to wake you up."

I flashed back to not being able to wake her up. "I actually do," I told her, my gaze steady on hers.

Comprehension showed in her eyes, and then acknowledgement.

I broke our bonding moment, because I was keenly aware of time ticking away. "Okay, I'm going to do this fast." Circling to the head of the bed, I almost took off my shoes but stopped myself.

"Ha! I'm not going there in my socks again," I declared.

"Do you have the spell?" Abby asked.

I sighed. "No, but I got back here without it. Hopefully I'll be able to go there without it too. I didn't use a spell to get there the first time," I added as the realization hit me. "I have no idea how I even ended up there."

Abby stood up and turned to face me. "Don't do this, Hazel. You don't know how all this magic stuff works. Let's get a witch to help us. Remember? That was the plan before you ended up in a coma. And we haven't even talked about how that happened."

She put her hands on her hips and gave me a disapproving look. "I'm guessing you broke your promise not to talk to him by yourself."

"I did," I admitted. "I'm sorry. I thought he needed my help."

She let her pointed look speak for her.

"This is different. Devon really does need my help." I put up my hand to stall her argument as she opened her mouth. "We don't have time to look for a witch first. I have to talk to him and tell him the plan so he can jump back in his body as soon as we get Lucius out of it. And this time you'll be here with me."

She snorted. "Yeah, that will be a lot of help. What can I really do if something goes wrong? *Nobody* could wake you up out of that coma, Hazel. Not me, or your parents, or even the doctors. And then you still didn't come out of it after we did the spell to come back. I was getting scared that you were gonna stay like that."

"I'm sorry I scared you, but I had to check on Devon. And it's a good thing I did, because he was hurt."

"Hurt?" she asked in alarm. "What happened? Is he okay?"

"He was when I left, but I don't know if he still is. We don't have time to get into what happened. I promise I'll tell you everything later, but I have to go before it gets dark."

Her eyes widened. "The monsters Lucius warned us about. He wasn't making that up to try to scare us, was he?"

"No," I admitted.

"Hazel," she said in admonishment and exasperation.

"Abby, please. I can't leave him stranded there."

She groaned. "Okayyy. But you better come back right away. Just tell him the plan and get out of there."

"Okay," I agreed. "Remember to look up churches while I'm gone."

I laid down on my bed as she hovered anxiously beside me. Closing my eyes so I could focus, I pictured the house instead of Devon. I was afraid if I envisioned him that I might end up going to Lucius by mistake.

Unlike with the spell, it wasn't instantaneous. I felt the power rising within me, maybe because I remembered it now. Lucius had taught me how to bring it forth, and I did. This time it was for me, and it transported me to the place I wanted to go.

At least I hoped it had. Pouring rain drenched me immediately before I even blinked my eyes open, and a relentless wind lashed at me. This was no gentle shower; it was a storm. I struggled to move against the wind just as lightning struck.

CHAPTER 15

t hit mere feet away from me, stopping me in my tracks. I screamed at the loud crack of thunder before I had even processed how close to death I had been. It rattled my whole body, and I stood there in shock as buckets of rain poured down on me.

Suddenly, there was a person in front of me. "C'mon," Devon yelled, grabbing my arm and dragging me behind him.

My feet moved automatically, following him to safety. He propelled me in front of him when we reached the porch steps and gave my butt a shove up them. Another crash of thunder sounded behind us, and I scrambled onto the porch in terror.

He was right behind me, sprinting toward the door and into the house. "Are you hurt?" he asked, inspecting me as I stood dripping rainwater onto the floor.

He was in a similar state, but he looked sexy while I probably looked like a drowned rat. "No," I answered him. "I'm okay. I was lucky. It didn't hit me."

"Lucky?" he exploded. "How long will it be before your luck runs out? Why the hell did you come back here? You finally made it back to your body, and then you come right back to this hellhole? What the hell is wrong with you?"

"You knew I got back to my body?" I asked in surprise.

His mouth compressed into an angry line. "I saw *him* visit you."

Concern altered his expression. "You shouldn't have let him know you knew it was him. Calling him out about the text wasn't smart. Now he knows you're onto him. Next time you see him, pretend like he's me. You can play it off like you were confused when you came out of your coma."

"The next time I see him, I'll have a priest with me," I declared. "I'm glad you can see what he's doing, because you have to be ready to get back into your body as soon as he's out."

"A priest? You're going to do an exorcism?" he asked, looking at me like I was crazy. "I was just being sarcastic when I said that. You know he's not really a demon."

"But he is," I said and told him about Lucius's demonic red eyes and his demon horse.

A horrified look slowly replaced the doubt on his face. "I actually summoned a demon?"

"That's what he looked like, and he's possessed your body, so..."

"I'm so sorry, Hazel. I screwed up, and you got caught up in my mistake. None of it should have ever affected you. Now you've got this psycho after you, and you've lost your memory—"

"I've got it back!" I interrupted him excitedly. "I remember everything!"

"You do? When did that happen?"

"When I woke up in the hospital. I knew who I was, and I knew my mom and dad, and I remembered my whole life."

"Oh, that's good," he said, sounding relieved. "At least it turned out okay for you."

"It will for you too," I promised him. "We're working on getting you out of here. Just be ready to go as soon he's out of your body. I don't know if he'll go back to hell or what, but don't give him a chance to get back in."

He shook his head, sending rain droplets flying from his wet hair. "It's too dangerous. The last time you stood in his way, he almost killed you. Leave him alone and stay away from him as much as you can. Go live your life and forget about all this."

"And leave you here? No way, that's not happening. You're getting your life back too."

"Maybe I don't want it back. Did you ever think of that? Maybe I *want* to stay here."

A crash of thunder rattled the windows, making me jump. Refocusing on the conversation, I said in disbelief, "By yourself? With no people anywhere? I know you don't mean that."

"Yes, because I'm so attached to people."

His words would have stung before he'd come here to find me and refused to leave when I'd been stuck here. But he couldn't fool me with sarcasm and his mask of indifference anymore. He had some sort of attachment to me whether he admitted it or not.

I didn't call him on it though, not yet. "What about your dad? You must miss—"

"My dad doesn't want me back," he cut in like that should be obvious to me. "His son isn't defective anymore. Now he's got a son he can be proud of and brag about to his friends."

"Don't say that about yourself! Nobody thinks that about you. I don't know why you've got that in your head, but your dad loves you and would never see you that way."

His harsh laugh held no amusement. "Then why is he making plans to send me to private school now that I can walk? Why is he having a birthday party for me for the first time since I was thirteen? I'll tell you why. It's because he doesn't have to be embarrassed by his handicapped son anymore."

He produced a smile that broke my heart. "Isn't that great? It's actually what I wanted when you think about it."

My hand had lifted to my mouth as he told me the terrible truth about his father. Tears sprang to my eyes as I thought about how he'd been treated after his tragic accident. Instead of being shown love and support, he'd been made to feel inferior to who he'd been before. No wonder he'd tried to use a spell to regain the ability to walk. He'd wanted his dad's approval and love. And now he was watching him give that to Lucius just because he wasn't in a wheelchair.

Anger began to burn in my belly. I dropped my hand as it rose up and burst from my mouth. "Fuck your dad!"

He raised his eyebrows and remarked, "He's a little old for you."

"I'm serious," I insisted, but he stopped my incoming rant about his father by closing the distance between us and grazing my bottom lip with his finger.

"I am too," he said. "Allow me to offer my services instead."

"Devon," I admonished him, but my voice was unsteady. My lip tingled where he had touched it, and I craved for him to press his lips to mine. I remembered what it felt like to kiss him, and I wanted to do it again.

The wild weather outside seemed to highlight the intimacy between us inside. Our wet clothes clung to us, heightening my awareness of our bodies. Devon was wearing the clothes he'd first arrived here in—jeans and a white t-shirt, which was now pretty much transparent. He looked even hotter than in the old-fashioned clothes he'd had on the last time I'd seen him soaking wet.

His dark eyes watched my mouth, stirring all the butterflies in my stomach. When his gaze met mine, his heated look drew me to him like a moth to the flame. We came together in a kiss that felt inevitable. I belonged with him, and every part of me knew it. Kissing him was magical and perfect, and I couldn't get enough.

I lost track of time and everything else. When his hand slipped lower to touch me through the wet fabric covering my chest, I moaned at the tantalizing sensation I'd never felt before. It emboldened him to ease the ache with a firmer touch and a light squeeze that had me kissing him harder. But when he started to pull my t-shirt up, my sense of modesty returned and broke the spell.

I stumbled back away from him, breathless and disoriented and still craving him. "What are you doing?" I panted.

His breathing was affected too, but he managed a sexy smile. "Getting you out of those wet clothes."

"Too soon," I said, surprising myself with the realization that I wanted to be with him that way—eventually. "It's not time for that yet."

His eyes burned into mine with an intensity that seemed to have more than passion behind it. "It's the perfect time. I can be everything you want right now."

"You've always been the guy I wanted," I admitted, feeling a twinge of guilt for Matt but not as much as I had before. Too much had happened since he died, and I couldn't deny my feelings for Devon anymore.

"But I can give you more," he said, stepping forward and picking me up by the waist.

He carried me to the door and set my back against it. I instinctively wrapped my legs around him for balance, and he pressed his body into mine as he captured my mouth in a hungry kiss.

Like all his kisses, it was hot. But I would have preferred to have my feet safely on the floor. This position felt precarious, and I was too off kilter to be able to completely get into it.

I tore my mouth from his and asked, "Can you put me down?"

He stared at me, appearing stunned by my request, but he did as I asked. "You didn't like that?" he questioned as he stepped back from me.

"I liked kissing you, but I'm not ready to have sex," I told him, hoping that he wouldn't reject me again because of that.

He blew out a frustrated breath. "I guess our timing sucks."

"It will be the right time one day," I assured him. "Once you're home and everything is back to normal, we could maybe go out on a date?"

My heart pounded after putting that out there. I'd basically just asked him out.

He hesitated, and my heart sank. "Maybe you could come visit me here. I know it's selfish of me to want that, and I wouldn't be able to take you anywhere, but the magic meal thing is still working. I woke up craving bacon and eggs, and they were on the kitchen table when I came downstairs. Tell me what kind of food you want, and I can have a gourmet meal ready for you. It might not be like going to a five-star restaurant, but I'll do my best."

My mood soared, and I beamed at him with what was probably too much enthusiasm. But I didn't care about playing it cool and hiding my happiness that he wanted to be with me. "Anywhere with you sounds good."

Wonder showed in his eyes as he searched mine, and then he stepped forward and wrapped his arms around me. Devon was hugging me, and I knew how special that was. He didn't show affection, but that was exactly what he was doing right now. I embraced him with all the love in my heart, and I knew that this was more than a crush.

"I love you," I told him.

He froze and slowly pulled back to look at me. I met his gaze straight on, not shying away from what I'd said. There were scarier things than admitting it, and I'd already faced them. Death, and monsters, and a demon. Being rejected wouldn't kill me.

I could see the doubt in Devon's eyes, and my anger for his father resurfaced. "I love you," I repeated, realizing that he hadn't heard that enough in his life.

"You do?" he asked with an uncertainty that broke my heart.

"Duh," I said, rolling my eyes. "Why do you think I'm here? For the memories?"

I snorted. "Get it? Amnesia joke."

Instinctively, I knew that this was the right approach to take with him. Too much intense emotion too fast would overwhelm him and make him withdraw from me.

My tactic worked, because he grinned at me. "I love you too," he said, still smiling.

My breath caught in my throat, holding there as I wondered if he meant it.

His expression turned serious, and he stared into my eyes for a moment, conveying the seriousness of his words. He pulled me close again for a shorter hug this time before the expressing of so much emotion became too much for him.

He cleared his throat as he let me go and stepped back. "You should get back before someone realizes you're gone."

"Yes," I agreed, but I wasn't worried about anything. I felt light as a feather, floating on pure happiness.

The most amazing and wonderful thing had happened. Devon loved me.

Swept up on the euphoria of that, I was sure that everything would work out perfectly for us. I'd already gotten my memory and my body back, and he would get his life back too. We would be together and live happily ever after.

"Do you have the spell to get back?" he asked.

"Don't need it," I replied happily. "I just picture where I want to go, and I'm there. You should try it too. I bet we never needed that spell in the first place. I didn't use it to get here the first time."

Realization flashed in his eyes. "You're right. I never thought about that."

"Me either. Until I was suddenly back in my body without knowing how I got there."

"I'm glad you got back," he said. "If it can only be one of us, I'm glad it's you."

"It will be both of us," I told him with the blissful confidence of a happy person. "Be ready to jump back in as soon as he's out."

"Hazel, leave him alone," he warned.

But I was too elated to argue with him. "Gotta go. Love you!"

I closed my eyes and pictured my familiar bed, and I was back on it instantly.

And I was ready to fight a demon for my man.

CHAPTER 16

was dying to tell Abby everything that had happened with Devon, but I had to help him first. "Did you find a priest?" I asked as soon as I opened my eyes.

"Thank God you're awake," she exclaimed. "Don't ever do that again!"

I sat up, marveling that my clothes were dry. So was my hair. It was like I'd never left this room. "Did my mom come up here? I'm sorry you had to cover for me."

"No, and thank God she didn't. Because you were in a coma again, Hazel! I shook you, and there was nothing. You didn't react at all. And then you didn't come back after a few minutes like you said you would. It was scary not knowing if you were okay."

I grinned, unable to help it. "I was better than okay."

Her eyes widened before she went off on me in exasperation. "Are you kidding me? You had me worried to death while you were over there hooking up with him?"

"We weren't hooking up; we were kissing." But my face got hot with the memory of him lifting me and pressing me against the door. That had been more than kissing. We'd done more than kiss. "And I'm sorry for scaring you. We got a little carried away."

She huffed. "Well, did you tell him the plan at least?"

"Yes. Did you look up churches?"

She grabbed her phone off my nightstand. "Yeah, and I think we should go to a Catholic church. The priest in the Exorcist was Catholic."

"Right, okay," I said switching gears to focus on defeating Lucius. "I've got to think of a way to get my mom to let me leave the house. I wish she'd gone to work today like my dad did."

"Maybe we could call the church instead," Abby suggested. "You can explain everything over the phone."

"I guess I'll have to. I just hope he doesn't think I'm crazy."

That turned out not to be the problem. Father Morris was more concerned with getting permission from Devon's father. I hadn't revealed anyone's actual name except my own. I'd told him that I thought a friend of mine was possessed by a demon.

"I can't do anything without the consent of the family."

"But his dad won't believe me!" I didn't actually know this for sure, but it was a strong possibility considering everything Devon had told me about him.

"Perhaps give him my number and let him know he can call me if he changes his mind. Even if he doesn't accept the possibility now, he might come around to it if his son starts showing more signs of possession."

He paused, and then said gently, "But Hazel, you need to consider other possibilities too. There is a chance that your friend is mentally ill rather than possessed. In my experience, that has sometimes been the case."

It hadn't occurred to me that he might think Devon was crazy. How discouraging that even a priest wasn't convinced. I couldn't let it defeat me though. Changing tactics, I asked, "Can you give me some tips on how to do an exorcism?"

His voice took on an urgency it hadn't had before. "Don't attempt to perform one on your own. I know you want to help your friend, but you could be putting yourself in danger. There's no telling how he'll react, whether he's possessed or not. He could become violent, putting you at grave risk. I urge you to let his father handle this situation."

I had no faith in that man to do anything to save Devon. Would he even try to help him if he knew where his son really was? Or would he prefer the demon that had taken over his body, only because he could walk? Yeah, I wasn't leaving it up to him.

"Um, okay. Thanks for listening, Father Morris."

"I wish I could have been more help, but give my number to his father, just in case he needs it. You're also welcome to attend service, and bring your friend if you're able to. God can offer you comfort in trying times."

I seriously doubted that I could convince Lucius to go to church. "Okay, thank you. Maybe we'll see you there sometime." I winced at telling a lie to a priest, but I'd said maybe, so that wasn't as bad as a definite promise to go.

After saying bye and ending the call, I looked at Abby, who'd listened to the entire conversation, since I'd had it on speaker. "We're on our own."

"Hazel," she replied in a warning tone. "You heard what he said. We can't do an exorcism by ourselves! How would we even know what to do? And how would we get him to sit still for it?"

She brought up good points, but I had no choice. Leaving Devon stuck in that other world was not an option. I would do whatever I had to do to get him back. I grabbed my phone to start looking up information about exorcisms just as a text notification went off. It was from Devon, or rather from Lucius pretending to be Devon.

I hope you are resting comfortably. I'd like to extend an invitation to you to attend my birthday celebration this Friday evening at 6:00 o'clock at my home. Dinner will be served, and I will introduce you to my father, as I should have done the last time you were here.

I showed it to Abby. "Looks like he's learned how to text."

She stared at it. "Are you sure he's not Devon?"

"Yes, I was just with him! Remember?"

"Oh, right." She glanced at me with a glum expression. "So, Lucius likes you too."

I snorted. "More like he's trying to get rid of me because I'm the only one who knows who he is. You know he tried to kill me. That's why I ended up in that other world."

"What?" she exclaimed. "He actually tried to murder you?"

"Well," I hedged, "he was trying to kill Devon, and I got in the way."

Her shoulders slumped, and the bleak look in her eyes matched her tone. "He's evil."

"Don't worry," I said, trying to rally her spirits. "He'll be gone soon, and Devon will be back."

I believed that with my whole heart, but Abby looked even more defeated when she got a text. "He wants me to bring you to his party."

"You don't have to go," I assured her.

"But you're going," she stated, giving me a hard look. "No matter what I say, you're still going—and you're doing an exorcism. You're not going to listen to Father Morris either."

"I have to! I have to save Devon. I love him."

She sighed and started tapping on her phone screen.

"What are you doing?" I asked in alarm.

"Telling him I'll bring you," she answered in annoyance.

"You don't have to do that. I can go by myself. You need to—"

"Shut up, Hazel," she snapped, cutting me off. "I'm going with you, and that's it."

I couldn't help the smile that broke free on my face as love and warmth radiated out of me. She was always there for me. "You're my best friend," I said, hoping she knew how much I meant it.

If her beaming smile was any indication, she did. Schooling her features into a mock stern expression, she pointed her finger at me. "And don't you forget it."

I snickered at her quip.

Her eyes widened. "Oh! I didn't mean to joke about that. I'm sorry!"

"Don't be. I've been joking about it too. It's fun!"

Her expression turned contemplative. "It was so weird when you didn't know me. You didn't recognize me at all."

I winced. "I'm sorry."

"It's okay; it was great just to see you were okay. The coma is the worst, so please don't do that again. I can't handle that anymore."

Her plea saddened me, because I knew I couldn't give her what she wanted. But maybe I could. If my exorcism plan worked, then I wouldn't need to return to the other world where Devon was trapped. I'd have him back without having to upset Abby.

"I'm staying right here," I said, because it was true for now. Swinging my legs over the side of the bed, I patted the space beside me. "Sit down, and let's catch up. Tell me what's been going on."

I brightened as I remembered something. "Oh! Did you go out with Kyle?"

She gave me a withering look. "No, I didn't go on a date while you were in a coma."

"Oh. Well, you can go now that I'm back."

She walked over to my dresser and randomly picked up a bottle of perfume before setting it down. "I don't know if I want to."

"Why not? I thought you liked him."

She turned to look at me directly. "Hazel, I—"

"Girls," my mom said, barging in without knocking. "I think that's enough for today. Hazel shouldn't overdo it."

"Overdo what?" I asked. "I'm just sitting here."

"I should go home," Abby said. "Mom let me stay home from school so I could see Hazel as soon as she got out of the hospital, but she told me not to stay too long. Thanks for letting me be here, Mrs. Guthrie."

"Of course," Mom said. "I hope you understand that Hazel needs to rest now."

"I'm not tired," I complained. "Let Abby stay a little longer."

But she was already headed for the hallway. "I'll talk to you tomorrow, Hazel. Have a good night!"

"It's afternoon," I muttered as I watched her flee my room.

Because that was what she was doing, even though she was walking instead of running. Her generic parting words telling me to have a good night indicated that too. She was throwing out polite pleasantries to get away from me as soon as possible. I thought back to the conversation Mom had interrupted and realized that Abby had been about to tell me something important.

But she'd apparently changed her mind. Otherwise, she would have given me a meaningful look when she said she'd talk to me tomorrow. Instead, she'd avoided looking at me as she left. Which meant that she was keeping a secret from me. But why? I was her best friend, and she should know that she could tell me anything.

Guilt crept in as I recalled how I had kept my crush on Devon a secret from her. Was that the kind of secret she was keeping from me? We had been talking about Kyle. Had she forgotten that I already knew she liked him? But we'd been talking about why she didn't want to go out with him. Did she now have a crush on someone else?

But who? There was no one new at school except...

Oh no! It couldn't be Lucius!

I closed my eyes with the realization that it was. She'd been impressed by his castle, and his room of stars. Honestly, I'd been enchanted by that room too—and by him playing bittersweet music on the piano. Good thing she hadn't heard him play the piano, but who knew how else he'd charmed her while I was away. I had to put a stop to this now before he broke her heart.

"Are you okay?" Mom asked. "Should I take you back to the hospital?"

I opened my eyes. "No, I'm fine. Can I borrow your bible?"

Confusion crossed her face. "Uh, sure."

Alarm quickly followed. "Did you have a near death experience?"

"No," I assured her. "Nothing like that. I just, um, wanted to look some stuff up."

"In the bible. Not on the internet." The disbelief was evident in her eyes, along with the suspicion that I wasn't telling her the truth, but she didn't call me out on it. "I'll get it for you."

She left my room, and I heard her walking down the hall to her and my dad's bedroom. She was gone a short time before I heard her walking back and saw her return with the bible I had requested.

"Thanks," I told her as she handed it to me.

"We could go to church when you feel better if you want," she said. "I'm sorry that we stopped going. I don't have any excuse except laziness."

She used to take me to Sunday school when I was a kid, but I had lost interest in it after elementary school. I'd complained that I didn't want to go, and Mom hadn't put up much of a fight about it. Especially since my dad had rarely gone to church with us.

"It's okay, Mom. I don't need to go. I just want to read a little bit of the bible."

"Okay, but if there's anything you want to tell me, you can. Don't assume that I won't believe you. Remember, I believed you when you told me about Svetlana. If I accepted you being able to talk to ghosts, then I'm open to whatever else you have to say about the supernatural."

She was so sincere that I was tempted to tell her, but I didn't have time right now. I had to find out all I could about exorcisms so I could do one as soon as possible and kick out the demon that had stolen Devon's body.

"I didn't meet Jesus, if that's what you're thinking," I quipped. *But I need His help.*

She smiled. "I still believe that He was watching over you. It's good that you're turning to the bible for answers. I'll leave you to it and go pray and give thanks again. Call me if you need me." She pulled her phone out of her pocket and held it up to show me. "I've got it on me so I can hear your call immediately."

I gave her a look conveying how ridiculous I thought that was. "I'll just yell for you like always."

"Don't strain yourself. Just call me on my phone."

I rolled my eyes. "Whatever. I'll call you if it makes you happy."

But the call I made after she left was to Lucius. It pained me to pretend that he was Devon, but I had to in order to set my plan in motion. "I am so sorry," I said immediately after his hello. "It was such a shock seeing you walk, but of course I'm happy for you!"

There was a beat of silence before he said, "You saw me walk in the other realm."

I liked that word realm, but I focused on what I had to do. "I thought that was a dream, and it threw me off when I saw you walking for real."

I took a quick breath and continued. "But now we're both okay, and I want to get back to normal. Could you pick me up and drive me to school tomorrow?"

His hesitation had me berating myself for my abrupt shift in conversation. I should have spent more time talking to him and worked my way up slowly to that request.

"Yes, I will drive you," he said in a stilted manner that gave away without a doubt that he wasn't Devon.

"Thanks," I replied. "Can you pick me up at 6:30?"

Another pause. "School starts at 7:30. I leave my home at 7:00 and arrive by 7:15. Do you require that much additional travel time?"

I forced myself to say, "I'd like to have some extra time with you before school. We could stop at the park and talk."

A beat of silence before he said, "Yes, we shall do that."

I'd been holding my breath while awaiting his answer, and I let it out in relief. "Okay. I'll see you in the morning."

"Yes," he said and hung up.

Because he didn't know phone etiquette. Because there were no phones in his realm. Because he wasn't Devon. Keeping that in mind, I texted him my address in case he didn't know where I lived.

I set to work researching exorcisms—and creeping myself out in the process. I wished that I didn't have to do this alone, and that I could have a priest with me.

But I'd faced this demon before, and this time I was prepared for him. I practiced the prayers I would say to cast him out until I had them memorized.

After a strained dinner with my parents, during which none of us knew what to say to each other, I took a shower and went to bed early. I considered a quick trip to see Devon, but I decided not to take the chance of my mom checking in on me and finding me in a coma. She'd never let me go to school if that happened.

I hoped that Devon would be ready to take his body back as soon as I got rid of Lucius.

It never occurred to me that I would fail.

The first thing that went wrong was that he wasn't alone.

I thought he was when I flung open the door. I'd been watching for his arrival in between bouts of arguing with my mom about going to school. She'd wanted me to stay home, but I'd insisted that I felt great.

"Devon is here to pick me up," I'd said as I'd raced to the door upon hearing a car pull into the driveway.

It wasn't his truck, but it was him striding up to my door. But it actually wasn't, because it was Lucius.

"Why are you leaving so early?" Mom complained.

I noticed that she was no longer saying I couldn't go. "So we can have time to talk before school. Things were a little weird yesterday at the hospital, and I wanted to make sure that we're okay."

She couldn't respond to that, because he was stepping up to the door. "I'll be right out," I told him. "I've just gotta grab my backpack."

I heard Mom invite him inside as I rushed to the living room sofa where I'd plopped down my backpack when I came downstairs. I hoped that inviting him in wasn't like inviting in a vampire. If only Mom hadn't gotten up to check on me, I might have gotten away before she was awake. I'd been planning to leave a note for my parents in the kitchen. My dad was still asleep, so at least I didn't have to deal with him too.

As I hurried back, Lucius was telling Mom about his birthday party. "Hazel has promised to attend with Abby."

"Oh, that's wonderful! Of course she'll be there."

"Yes," I agreed, remembering to smile at him like I thought he was actually Devon. "I can't wait." *For you to be gone and Devon to be back.*

I gave my mom a quick peck on the cheek, which wasn't something I normally did. But being without her had made me appreciate her more. "Bye, Mom. See you later."

"Go to the nurse's office if you don't feel well. I'll come pick you up if you need to go home."

"I will. Don't worry." I started for the door before she could hold me up any longer.

Lucius followed me out, and I was dismayed to see a man get out of the car as we approached it. I halted in my tracks. "Who's that?"

"My chauffeur," he said, placing his hand at the small of my back to guide me along.

My feet moved automatically, but my mind was stalled. My plan was in ruins. It hinged on us being alone in his car, but now this man was here opening the door for me. Why was he here? Devon had never had a chauffeur before.

The answer came to me in the next instant. *Because Lucius didn't know how to drive.*

There were no cars in his world. That was why he rode a horse to get around.

As I sat down in the backseat, my mind scrambled for a way to salvage my plan. I couldn't waste this opportunity now that I had it. I'd wanted to do it in the car, but maybe being trapped in there with a demon wasn't the best idea, now that I thought about it. Being outside where I could run away if I had to would probably be better. I also wasn't going to risk putting the driver in danger.

My heart sped up when Lucius sat down beside me in the backseat, but I tried to calm my nerves. We were momentarily alone, and it was too close and confined. "We need to park at the golf course," I told him, my unsteady voice giving away how nervous I was. "The entrance to the park is there."

The driver got into the front seat, instantly relieving some of the tension with his presence. Lucius relayed my information to him, and we were soon pulling out of my driveway. Lucius reached over and tried to take my backpack, but I clutched it to me protectively.

"I'll set it on the front seat for you so you won't have to hold it on your lap."

"No thanks. I like holding it."

His eyes fixed on my backpack with a suspicious look, and I held my breath, waiting to see if he would try to pry it out of my grip. His gaze lifted to mine, and I tensed, bracing myself for an attack. Would the driver help me, or would he be loyal to the son of the man who was paying him? Should I fling myself out of the car? I'd be risking injury, but it might be worth it to escape.

"Have you taken ill?"

I blinked out of my panicked indecisiveness and saw Lucius watching me with a wary expression. "What?" I asked in confusion.

"Do you need medical attention? Should we return to your home and alert your mother?"

He was offering to take me home? The realization that he wasn't going to attack me roused me from my disoriented state. I'd let paranoia derail me, but I snapped back on track. "No, I'm fine. I just got...um, a little dizzy. But I'm fine now."

"Like in the ballroom," he said and frowned. "Do you have these episodes often? Perhaps you need medical tests to discover the cause."

A demon was concerned about my health? This was bizarre. But it was probably an act to make me believe that he was Devon.

Something nagged at my mind, and it suddenly sprang to the forefront. He'd mentioned the ballroom, but I hadn't been there with Devon. That had been Lucius.

He'd just given himself away!

I kept my expression neutral, careful not to let it show on my face. "I'm okay. Just need some fresh air. It will be good to be outside in the park before we have to be stuck sitting in a classroom."

This was good. I'd given him an even better reason for why I wanted to go to the park. Now I just needed to follow through on my plan when we got there.

"There are so many people at school," he said, amazement in his voice.

Another dead giveaway that he wasn't Devon. Although I'd been a bit overwhelmed when I returned to this world. And I'd only been gone for days. What must it be like for him after living without people for years?

I caught myself and hardened my heart. I couldn't let down my guard and start empathizing with him. He was a demon. And he had stolen Devon's body and his life.

"And so much homework," I quipped, sticking to safe subjects so I wouldn't let anything slip myself. "I probably have tons to catch up on."

"They will accommodate you and give you ample time to complete your assignments. That is what they did for me."

"That's good," I said.

We lapsed into a short silence, but it was so awkward that I rushed to fill it. "So, you're having a party."

"Yes. It will be a grand affair, with all the best people attending."

"The best people?" I asked, assuming he meant his old friends from the popular crowd.

"High society," he clarified. "My father wants me to get reacquainted with their offspring before I begin attending private school with them."

He misinterpreted my look of dismay. "Don't fret about your lack of wealth. You and Abby are my guests and shall be treated accordingly."

"Right, we'll fit right in with all your rich friends." My sarcastic reply masked what was really bothering me. Devon's father was rapidly making big changes to Devon's life, and Lucius was going along with all of them.

"It is not your place to fit in. By my side you shall stand above them. They are coming to see me, after all, and you are with me."

His confidence astonished me. Yes, Devon had it too, acting like nobody at school measured up to him. But Lucius was talking about being the center of attention in a room full of strangers he'd never met.

Or maybe he had. Did he have Devon's memories from before Devon summoned him? There was so much I wanted to ask him, but I couldn't since I was pretending that I didn't know he was Lucius.

Luckily, it didn't take long to get to the golf course. This early, there were no other cars in the parking lot. I pointed out the entrance to the park and suggested we go for a short walk. Anxiety hit me anew as I got out of the car. This was it. I was about to go up against a demon.

"You can leave that in the car," he said.

I slung my backpack over one shoulder so I could take it off quickly when I needed to. "I've got water bottles in case we get thirsty."

"You said it's a short walk. Surely, we can wait to quench our thirst until we return to the car."

"Let's not waste time arguing. We don't want to be late for school," I said and started for the park entrance.

As I'd hoped, he joined me. But then he played the gentleman. "Allow me to carry it for you."

He reached out for it, and I sidestepped away from him as I held tightly to the strap looped over my shoulder. "I've got it."

This time he came out and asked me directly. "What do you have in there that you don't want me to see?"

I was about to deny it, but I realized that I could use this instead of my lame plan to declare that I was thirsty after a few minutes of awkward small talk. "I'll show you, but let's get further into the park so your driver doesn't see. It's private, and I don't want to show it to a stranger."

He looked intrigued now rather than suspicious. "Alright, proceed."

My anxiety ramped up as we resumed our walk and entered the park. The trees along the trail were vibrant with colorful autumn leaves. Nothing like the creepy barren trees in Lucius's world. He gazed at them in appreciation, and he was so human that it was hard to believe that a demon lurked inside him.

"This world is so beautiful," he marveled.

A flash of that same bittersweet feeling that I'd felt when I heard him play his music hit me in the chest. I struggled to push it aside and harden my heart. I couldn't feel any sympathy for him if I was going to cast him out of Devon's body.

After I was sure we were out of sight of the driver, I halted and pulled my backpack off my shoulder. I didn't want to get too far away from the parking lot, because Devon couldn't walk the trail. He'd need help getting to the car.

Lucius had walked ahead a little bit and had stopped and turned to face me.

"I'll show you now," I told him, my nerves coming back in full force as I unzipped the backpack.

Dropping it on the ground after pulling out the bible, I flipped open the holy book to the first passage I had saved with a bookmark. I recited the Lord's prayer and glanced up to see the effect it had on Lucius.

He had crossed his arms over his chest and was standing there looking at me with an amused expression.

I looked back down at my bible and read the Hail Mary prayer from the slip of paper I'd placed there along with my bookmark. Turning to the next bookmarked page, I read the Athanasian Creed I had written down on a piece of paper and placed there.

When I glanced up at Lucius again, I saw that he hadn't moved or changed his expression. He wasn't affected at all.

I closed the bible and held it in one hand while I dug in my pocket with the other and pulled out my old cross and necklace. I'd worn it as a child, but the chain was too small for me now.

I brandished it at him and recited the verse I had memorized. "In the name of Jesus Christ, I command you to come out of him."

His only reaction was to raise his eyebrows at me like he was questioning my sanity.

In desperation, I went with movie lines. "Be gone, spawn of Satan!"

He burst out laughing, unfolding his arms to point a finger at me indicating how funny I was.

This was not the response I had expected, and humiliation swept over me. Frustration was next, and I flew at him and shoved my cross in his face, hoping to drive him out that way. He stopped laughing, but he only looked startled. His skin didn't burn from the contact, and he didn't let out an unholy shriek of pain or fear. He simply stared at me with Devon's dark eyes.

I was the one who shrieked as I smacked his chest with the bible. "Go back to hell!"

His expression flattened. "I didn't come from hell."

"I saw you," I said. "You're a demon."

He blew out an exasperated breath. "I'm not a demon."

"But I saw you! You had red eyes and *claws*."

He looked away. "I never wanted you to see me like that."

Had that been shame in his eyes? I pushed aside that thought and said in a hard tone, "You mean your demon side?"

He sighed. "How can I prove to you that I'm not a demon?"

"Go to church."

He nodded. "Alright, I will. Provide me the address and the time, and we shall attend together."

I eyed him suspiciously, wondering what kind of trick this was. I had expected him to refuse.

He glanced at his watch. "We should return to the car if we are to arrive at school on time."

"It's only five minutes away," I told him, but I put the bible back inside my backpack so I could pull out my phone to check the time.

"Shall we?" he said, sweeping his arm out toward the direction we had come from.

I put my phone away and zipped up my backpack, starting to sling it over my shoulder but abruptly dropping it. "Wait! What about Devon? You have to leave his body. He needs to come back!"

His expression soured. "Forget him. He's better off where he is."

"How can you say that? He's all alone."

His gaze fixed on mine. "And I wasn't?"

That truth hit me hard, and I had no comeback to it.

"I was there for years, Hazel, and your precious Devon didn't spare a thought to me. Pine after that wretch if you want to, but don't plead his case to me."

He jerked my backpack up off the ground and strode past me. I stood there reeling from my utter failure and conflicted feelings. I didn't want to feel compassion for Lucius, but it was hard not to when I imagined his lonely existence. But that didn't mean that it was right to leave Devon to that fate.

But I didn't know how to get him out of it. "I'm sorry, Devon," I said in case he was here listening. "I'll think of a new plan."

I had no choice but to leave in defeat and trudge after Lucius.

How was I going to get Devon back now?

CHAPTER 18

People took notice of us arriving at school together. Especially since we pulled up right at the front entrance and got out of the back seat. I'd flung open my door before the driver could get to it, but students still saw that we'd been driven there by a chauffeur.

It felt ridiculously over the top and pretentious. I wasn't shy, but I also didn't like to show off and try to impress people. I knew that wasn't what Lucius was doing, but that was how it would look to everyone. They had no reason to think that he didn't know how to drive, since they'd seen Devon driving lots of times. They had no clue that he wasn't Devon.

Abby was the only other person who knew that, and she happened to be one of the people who saw us arrive. I hurried toward her, so glad that I had someone I could talk to about this.

But her eyes narrowed at me as I approached her. "Why are you holding a cross? Did you try to do it by yourself? Oh my God, Hazel! Are you insane?"

I glanced down at my hand. I hadn't realized that I was still clutching my necklace with the cross dangling from it.

"So, you are involved in this foolishness," Lucius said as he came up beside me. "I should have known."

Abby turned her ire from me to him. "What's that supposed to mean?"

"Only that you follow Hazel in all things."

She sucked in a breath like he'd landed a punch, and I glanced at him to see a mocking expression on his face that quickly cleared. He clenched his jaw and dragged his attention away from her. He stiffly handed me my backpack and strode to the entrance with angry steps, ignoring everyone who greeted him.

I turned my bewildered gaze to Abby. "What was that about?"

She exhaled and then slowly inhaled in an apparent attempt to calm herself. "Nothing."

"Hazel!" Emily exclaimed as she bounded up to me and gave me a hug. "I knew you'd be okay!"

I was glad to see her back to her usual happy self again. She'd been so despondent the night Abby collapsed. "Thanks," I said as I slipped the chain and cross into my pocket.

She nodded toward it with a bright smile. "God worked a miracle for you too. I knew if He could make Devon walk that He could bring you out of your coma."

The irony! She thought that God was responsible, and I thought that a demon had possessed his body. "Yeah, that's amazing. So, how have you been?"

"Good. I've started going to church more. I'm trying to get Devon to go, but he's said no so far."

"He told me he'll go."

I regretted it the instant I said it. Involving Emily in this mess had not been my plan, but she exclaimed in delight and invited me to go too. She was under the impression that he had decided to go to her church.

I supposed it didn't matter which church I took him to, so we might as well make her happy. But what if he had some kind of demonic reaction to being there?

We had to get to our classes, so I put off worrying about that. What was more important was thinking of a new plan to get Lucius out of Devon's body. I had no idea why the exorcism had failed, but it was obvious that I had to try something else. But what else was there?

It was hard not to feel discouraged. I should have been relieved to be out of my coma and to have my memory back. And a part of me was, but there was another part of me that had been left behind with Devon in that other world.

I watched Lucius in our first class, wondering if he could have fooled me if I hadn't known that he wasn't Devon. He was identical to him in looks, but there was something missing. Something intangible that drew me to Devon like a moth to a flame.

It had always been there, from the first moment I saw him. Love at first sight, which some people would say was merely attraction. But if that was the case, then why didn't I feel it with Lucius? He looked exactly the same as Devon, but there was nothing drawing me toward him.

So, it had to be something beyond looks. But what? It couldn't be personality, because I had known nothing about Devon when I'd had that intense reaction to him the first time I'd seen him. The answer came from the back of my mind, but it was hard to believe, despite the fantastical things I'd experienced.

He was my destiny.

If I said that aloud, I would cringe. It was in the same category as believing in fairy tales and Santa Claus. Something that you outgrew as you matured past the kid stage and had to deal with reality. Magic wasn't real, and neither were soulmates.

Except, magic *was* real. I'd experienced it myself and even cast spells.

My mind caught on that thought. Spells. Of course! I needed a spell to cast out Lucius and get Devon back.

Unfortunately, the only one I could find was in Latin. The person who had posted it warned that that the demon would try to interrupt you, so you needed to have it memorized. How was I going to do that when I couldn't even pronounce the words?

"Ow!"

I looked up from my phone to scowl sideways at Abby, who had just kicked my leg. She scowled back at me. "Sarah asked you how you're feeling."

I glanced sheepishly at Sarah. I wasn't paying attention to my friends, because I was too distracted with secret things I couldn't tell them about. "Sorry. I'm good. How are you?"

"I'm so glad you're okay," she said, making me feel even guiltier. "I couldn't believe it when I heard you were in a coma. What did the doctors say? What caused it?"

"They don't really know. They tried to tell me it was stress," I said derisively. "But c'mon, that's ridiculous. Lots of people have stress, and they don't end up in a coma."

"But you've had more than most. First with losing Matt, and then with what happened with Abby. Even though she was okay, you probably had flashbacks to the day Matt died. I can understand how it overwhelmed you with stress."

Now the guilt was a knife twisting in my gut. So much had happened since Matt died, that I'd barely thought of him lately. He didn't have anything to do with my stress level or with the reason I'd been in a coma.

My eyes strayed to Lucius, who was sitting with the popular crowd. He'd invited me to join him, but I'd refused. I glared at him now as I thought about how he was the cause of all my problems. He was the reason that Devon wasn't here where he belonged. He was also responsible for zapping me into a coma...

The realization hit me with sudden force, and excitement bubbled up within me. Lucius had taken power from me and combined it with his own to defeat Devon—something that he couldn't do on his own. So, if Devon and I combined our power, we should be able to defeat Lucius!

The only problem was that Devon wasn't here to help me do that. But maybe I didn't need him here physically. He'd told me that he was able to travel here in spirit and see what Lucius was doing.

And wasn't that what he'd done when he'd intruded on me when I'd reached out to Lucius? *With my mind.* Because I'd been alone in my room until my mind transported me to a place where I could see and interact with Devon and Lucius.

We could all do it! We didn't need to be in the same physical place. But did we need to be in the same world? Last time, Devon had been right here in Salem. Now he was...

I still didn't actually know where he was.

"Hazel, how's it going?"

Pulled out of my reverie by the sound of my name, I saw that Kyle was standing beside me. I smiled up at him. "Good. How have you been?"

I glanced over at Abby to see her reaction to him, but she was staring down at her food. Kyle's gaze also slid toward her before it returned to me with a fake happy expression. "I'm good. Just wanted to let you know I'm glad you're okay."

"Thanks," I said, but he was already turning and walking away.

I looked at Abby, wondering what had happened between them. I should have asked her yesterday, but I'd been too giddy about being in love with Devon. I got a bit of that same rush right then just thinking about it.

But I had promised myself that I would be a better friend—right before I'd broken my promise to Abby not to contact Lucius alone. I winced, wanting to apologize to her, but not being able to talk about it in front of the rest of our friends.

What I did do was vow to myself to be as good of a friend to her as she was to me. I was going to listen to her and include her in everything. No more secrets, and no more rushing off to do things by myself.

Which is what she yelled at me for as soon as she had a chance after school. "What were you thinking doing an exorcism by yourself? You were supposed to wait for me!"

"I'm sorry, but it didn't work anyway. I even brought a bible with me and said prayers, but nothing happened."

She huffed. "Well, at least you had his driver there with you. But—"

She cut herself off as she caught my grimace. "The driver wasn't there? Then where did you do it?"

I winced, bracing myself for her reaction. "The woods."

"You went to the woods by yourself with someone you thought was a demon! Are you crazy?"

I glanced around to see if any of my neighbors were outside to hear us, but there was no one. We were walking up my driveway after taking the school bus home. Lucius had offered to give us a ride, but we'd turned him down. I didn't want to accept favors from him when he'd stolen Devon's body. This morning had been different, because I'd been on a mission.

Since I'd promised my mom I'd come straight home after school, Abby had decided to come over so we could talk. "I just wanted to get

Devon back as soon as possible," I explained to her. "I had protection with the bible and the cross."

"He still could have attacked you. In that movie, the demon attacked the priest."

"Well, Lucius didn't. He just laughed at me. It was kind of embarrassing," I admitted.

She stomped up the porch steps. "He's such an asshole! He acted like a gentleman when we were in his castle, but he's a total asshole!"

She'd called him that twice during her short rant, and she stood fuming as I walked up beside her to unlock the door. "What is that about? What happened between you and him?"

Her head whipped toward me. "What?" she exclaimed with a panicked expression. "Nothing! I'm mad at him for what he did to you —and Devon."

Yeah, I wasn't buying that. She was clearly hiding something from me, and she seemed afraid to tell me about it. But why?

As we entered the house, I closed the door behind us and turned to confront her.

CHAPTER 19

opened my mouth but stopped before I spoke. I'd vowed to be a better friend, and that meant respecting Abby's feelings instead of demanding an explanation. That wasn't the way to get her to open up to me. I needed to wait until she was ready to tell me on her own, so I changed the subject.

"Come sit down and tell me how you've been," I said as I started toward the living room.

Abby followed my lead and plopped down on the couch beside me, visibly relaxing now that I wasn't questioning her about Lucius. "I've been good except for worrying about you. Thank God Devon left that spell book open so I could find out you were okay. Otherwise, I would have been as freaked out as your parents."

I winced. "I really put them through it. I've never seen my dad like that. He looked like he hardly slept at all."

"He really loves you," she said with a soft smile.

She always got like that whenever she heard about someone being a good dad. Probably because her biological father wasn't one. It reminded me how much I took mine for granted. Abby appreciated her stepfather more most of the time than I did my dad. I loved him, of course, but it wasn't something I gave much thought to except for on his birthday and Father's Day.

"Yeah," I acknowledged, but I still felt a bit uncomfortable to dwell on that with her. "But now he wants me to see a psychiatrist." I rolled my eyes.

She gaped at me. "You told him about the spell and the castle and everything?"

"Of course not. But the doctor thinks that stress might have caused my coma. Obviously, I couldn't tell him the truth."

She dropped her gaze from mine and then glanced up with a hesitant look. "It could be part of it. You *have* been through a lot."

I shook my head. "No, it was Lucius. It happened when he zapped me with his power—after he stole some of mine."

She was startled. "He stole your power? How?"

"He tricked me into giving it to him," I admitted sheepishly. "He said he needed my help to escape. Remember, I thought that Devon had him trapped somewhere."

And then I realized that it was true. "I guess he did in a way. But it was for a good reason. Lucius tried to kill him, and now he's stolen his body."

"But how is that even possible?" she exclaimed. "And why would his twin do that? Where is *his* body? Why wouldn't he just go back to it?"

It dawned on me how far behind she was, because I'd been in too much of a rush to catch her up on everything. Meanwhile, she'd been helping me without knowing what she was getting into. It wasn't fair to her.

"He's not Devon's twin, and he doesn't have a body."

She stared at me. "What do you mean he doesn't have a body? Everyone has a body until they die."

Her eyes widened. "Are you saying he's a ghost?"

I shook my head. "No. He's..."

I hesitated as I grappled with how to tell her without revealing something too personal about Devon. I knew that he wouldn't want me telling anyone about how he'd tried to heal his legs. That was a touchy subject for him.

"Uh, Devon did a spell when he was thirteen, and it went wrong."

Her eyes instantly filled with compassion and understanding. "He tried to bring back his brother," she said, jumping to the same conclusion I had.

"So, um, he somehow created Lucius." As I said it, I realized that it was true. He hadn't summoned Lucius, because Lucius hadn't existed. Or had he? I was still confused about that. In essence, Devon had tried to bring back his old self—the person he had been before the accident.

But was that who he had been? I hadn't known him then, so I couldn't say. All I knew was that I preferred *my* Devon. He was the one I had fallen in love with. Lucius seemed like some warped version of him.

"Then he's not his twin," Abby stated. "And he doesn't have a body because Devon created him."

She looked me straight in the eye. "How do you create a person, Hazel?"

I shrugged and replied helplessly, "I don't know."

"How does a person not have a body?" she demanded. "What *is* he?"

I was tempted to tell her then, to spill Devon's secrets. But that still wouldn't have explained what Lucius actually was. He claimed to be a version of Devon, but people were unique individuals. How could there be different versions of them?

"I don't know," I repeated with a heavy sigh. "I thought he was a demon, but he had no reaction when I touched him with the cross. I didn't have holy water, but I don't think it would have made a difference either. Plus, he said he'd go to church with me. It's looking like we won't get rid of him that way."

"So, he's not a demon," she said, looking relieved.

I flashed back to his demonic red eyes, but that had been in his world. Maybe he was normal here in our world, inside Devon's body. Maybe that made him less powerful, I thought, getting excited by that idea.

But I held it in so that I could focus on Abby first before I got carried away with my new plan. "Anyway, what happened with you and Kyle? You seemed kind of tense when he stopped by our table today."

"No, I wasn't," she immediately denied.

I suppressed my urge to insist that she was, and to pry into the reason. "Okay, well, finish telling me what you were saying about him yesterday before my mom interrupted us."

She shrugged. "There's really nothing to tell. I just decided not to go out with him."

I waited with an expectant look. "Because…"

She sprang up and took a few steps away from me. "Because it's not…it's not…right."

"Why wouldn't it be…wait! It's not because he kissed me in middle school, is it? That was just a stupid game."

"No, it's not that."

"Then what?" I asked. "I know he likes you, and you said that you like him too."

"I did, but—"

"Did?" I interrupted in consternation. "What did he do? He said something stupid, didn't he?"

"No, he's been really sweet. It's me. I'm not…"

"Ready?" I supplied. "Maybe you're just nervous. I know that going on your first date can be kind of scary, but it'll be fun."

"I'm not scared," she stated, and it sounded like truth instead of denial. "Kyle is a good guy, and he doesn't deserve to be second-best. I'm not going to do that to him."

"Second-best?" I questioned, completely confused. "What do you mean?"

Instead of answering, she said, "My biological father has a son, and I guess he's really proud of him. He posts pictures of him all the time. Anyone would think that he's a great dad."

I gaped at her. "You have a brother? When did you find this out?"

She appeared startled by my question. "A brother?" she repeated like it didn't make sense.

"If he's your father's son, then he's your brother. Right?"

She stared at me for a moment and then deflated. "He is. I didn't even think of it that way. I was just so mad when I saw those pictures. This whole time, I imagined him single and dating a bunch of women. Because that's what he told my mom when she left him, that he should have never gotten married and had a kid."

She laughed derisively. "But it turns out that he didn't want a daughter, because his son is only a year younger than me, and he hasn't been a deadbeat dad to him."

"He's an idiot," I said, getting angry. "He doesn't even deserve a great daughter like you."

She gave me a weak smile. "Thanks, Hazel."

"I'm serious! You're a much better daughter than I am—and a much better friend. I'm sorry I've been so caught up in my stuff that I didn't even give you a chance to tell me all this. When did you find out?"

"No, it's not your fault. I could have told you, but I didn't want to talk about it yet. I found out when I was bored in the hospital. I decided to look him up to see what his life is like. I was even thinking about sending him a message. Something like: Hey, asshole, I almost died."

She huffed a laugh. "Like he would even care."

"Forget him. What about your brother? I bet he doesn't know about you. Are you going to contact him?"

She sighed. "I don't know. Maybe. I'll have to think about it."

I stood up and went to her. "I'll go with you to meet him if you want. I can sit in the car or go in with you. Whatever you want."

She pulled me in for a hug. "Thanks, Hazel. You're the best."

Half of me soaked up her praise while the other half cringed. I'd hurt people—not on purpose, but because I'd been thoughtless and reckless. I wanted to be better. I *needed* to be better.

I would start with including Abby in the planning stage and asking for her opinion. "So," I said as I pulled back to look at her, "I want to know what you think of Plan B."

CHAPTER 20

stared at the destruction in disbelief. A huge, gaping hole yawned wide in the middle of the field of grass. The tree line that was beyond it was gone. I could see all of this because thick streaks of lightning were constantly flashing across the sky.

There was something wrong about that, but I couldn't pinpoint it at first. Then I realized that it wasn't one flash of lightning at a time. There were two and sometimes three simultaneously streaking across the dark sky and lighting up the night. The deafening thunder rattled my bones, and I ran for shelter.

Luckily, the house was intact, and I burst inside, immediately shutting and locking the door behind me. Only then did I realize that it had been unlocked. That's when I remembered the monsters. I'd been so excited to tell Devon the plan that I'd given no thought to the fact that it was night, and that the monsters might get me. I was so lucky that they weren't there. I could have teleported right into the midst of them and gotten mauled by their teeth and claws.

I shuddered and pushed that horrible thought aside. "Devon?" I called out, but my voice was drowned out by the relentless booms of thunder.

Seeing that he wasn't anywhere on this floor, I went upstairs and found him standing by the bedroom window, staring out at the constant flashes of lightning.

"You should get away from the window," I said anxiously. "I don't think it's safe to be so close to it when there's lightning."

He whirled and stormed up to me. "You're telling me what's safe? You know what's not safe? Going off into the woods with a demon and trying to do an exorcism! What the hell were you thinking?"

"I wasn't sure if you saw that."

"Yes, I saw it. You almost gave me a heart attack!"

I winced. "I'm sorry. I was trying to help you. But as you saw, I failed."

He expelled a breath. "I told you to let it go. Stop putting yourself in danger—please. I can't stand the thought of something happening to you."

The happiness in my heart spilled over into a smile on my face. Knowing that he cared about me was the best. But he needed to understand that it went both ways. "And I can't stand what he's doing to you. He has no right to steal your life and keep you trapped here."

He gazed at me with a mixture of wonder and tenderness in his eyes as he lifted his hand to cup my chin and stroke my cheek with his thumb. "I love you," he said before giving me a sweet, tender kiss.

It cocooned me in a warm, wonderful feeling. "I love you," I told him as he pulled back with a soft smile.

A crash of thunder jolted me as it rattled the window. "What if it hits the house?"

"It'll be okay, but you should probably get back."

I saw right through his attempt to reassure me. The fact that he was urging me to leave gave it away. He was worried too about it being unsafe here. "We should do the plan now."

"What plan?"

"You didn't hear me tell Abby about it?" I asked, only then realizing that would mean he might have heard everything we'd talked about.

"No." His expression darkened as he explained, "I'm only able to see you and hear you when you're with him. I'm limited to following him around—as much as I can stand it."

My heart hurt for him having to helplessly watch Lucius living *his* life. "We can stop him," I said, hoping that I was right. "If we combine our power, then you can hit him with it and knock him out of your body. Like Lucius knocked me out of mine."

"You mean when he almost killed you, and you ended up in a coma?" He shook his head. "I'm not doing that."

"I ended up here," I reminded him. "And with amnesia. It would be perfect if he forgot about you and never bothered you again. You don't actually have to kill him."

A harsh laugh burst forth from him. "You think I care if I kill him? I'm worried about *you*. Maybe you ended up in a coma because he took your power. Or maybe that was what caused your amnesia."

"No, that happened because he blasted me with all that power."

"How do you know?" he challenged. "What if the memory loss was a result of him draining your power? And what if doing it again makes it permanent?"

I stared at him in dismay. That horrible possibility hadn't occurred to me.

"We have no way of knowing, do we? You're just assuming it will work in your favor. I assumed the same thing when I did that damned spell after my accident, and I was so wrong. I'll never make that mistake again."

"But we have to do something! You can't stay here forever."

"It's not so bad," he said. "Especially since the monsters are gone."

"They are?"

He nodded.

"What happened to them?" I asked and immediately had a thought. "Maybe they fell in the hole."

"No, that happened today, but they weren't here last night either."

Suspicion sparked in my mind. "Neither was Lucius. Do you think that's a coincidence?"

"It could be," he said, but his gaze slid away from mine.

I could tell that he didn't believe that, and I didn't know why he wasn't saying so. If the monsters were connected to Lucius, then their absence was the only good thing about him not being here.

The horrific thought followed immediately after that conclusion. Were the monsters in our world now? Had he brought them with him?

"Do you think they followed him?" I asked aloud.

Devon ran a hand through his hair. "I think you probably would have heard about it by now if they had. Just to be on the safe side though, don't go outside at night for a few days."

"What about everyone else? I don't want anyone to get hurt. I have to warn people!"

"They won't believe you, Hazel. They'll think you're crazy."

"But what if someone gets attacked?"

"Then they'll know it's real, and then you would have another problem. They'll want to question you about how you knew and about this place. They'll take you away to some top-secret facility, and who knows if anyone will ever see you again."

I huffed out a disbelieving laugh. "That sounds like the plot of some movie."

He gave me a deadpan look. "And magically transporting to another world doesn't?"

He had a point. Unbelievable things had already happened to me. So, I shouldn't be so quick to rule out being kidnapped by the government.

I was abruptly shaken out of my thoughts. Devon propelled me to the doorway as the floor shook beneath our feet. Another earthquake!

"We need to get outside," I said, although that didn't seem much safer with the thunder and lightning.

"No time. Go back to your body now."

"I'm not leaving you."

"Damn it, Hazel, go!"

We stood facing each other in the doorframe. I looked back at him stubbornly as he glared at me. It kept the panic at bay as objects crashed to the floor and the house swayed like it might topple over.

When it stopped, there was a jagged crack in the wall running from beneath the window all the way across to the corner of the room. Devon went to inspect it, and I followed him with tentative steps.

A loud rumble began outside, and we both stared out the window as the ground split open in a long fissure that I thought was going to reach the house. My heart thundered as I watched it racing toward us. It stopped just a few feet away, and I stood there stunned.

The ground had just literally opened up in front of me. It was like this world was falling apart.

The realization struck, and I recalled Lucius telling me that this was his world. I turned to Devon in shell-shocked horror. "It's because he's not here."

"You need to go home," he said.

"No, you don't understand. It's falling apart because he left. He said this was his world, and maybe it really is. Like, it can't exist without him."

Devon didn't react to that theory. Didn't scoff and dismiss it. Didn't think about it with a doubtful expression. Didn't have a dawning look of realization on his face.

Because he already knew.

And he was urging me to go home, because he knew that he was running out of time. And he was going to send me back without telling me.

"What the hell?" I exploded at him. "Are you fucking kidding me? We're doing it! I'd rather lose my memory again than have you *die*."

His implacable expression brought back my panic. He wasn't going to change his mind about this.

"I'd rather have you remember me," he said.

His words held a bittersweet finality that tugged at my heart while also scaring me. Because it sounded like he was saying goodbye.

He slayed me when he added, "You're the only one who sees me as more than a guy in a wheelchair."

"That's not true," I said in a desperate attempt to get through to him. "All the popular people like you. You're the one who decided you didn't want to be part of their crowd anymore. You're the one who walked away."

I winced at my poor choice of words, but he didn't notice.

"They only accepted me because of who my father is. They wouldn't have bothered if I was just a regular guy."

I couldn't argue with that, because they were all about image and status. But it still hurt my heart when he added, "And they like Lucius better because he can walk."

Before I could respond to that, he stepped closer and said, "You need to go back, Hazel."

He bent to kiss me, and I made my decision in a split second. Stepping back from him, I replied, "I'm going to blast him with all I've got tomorrow at his party. I hope you'll combine your power with mine and help me, but I'll do it by myself if I have to. Be ready to take your body back."

I looked him directly in the eyes and added, "That's when I'll kiss you."

My bold move made me blush, but I hoped he wanted it enough to fight for it. Not just a kiss, but to be with me. "I love you," I reminded him.

I closed my eyes and then peeked one open. "You don't need the spell. Just focus on where you want to go."

Proceeding to prove it to him, I pictured my room and was instantly drawn back into my body. The silence was very noticeable after the constant crashes of thunder. Anxiety twisted my stomach into knots as I wondered how long Devon had before Lucius's world completely fell apart. I prayed for him to be safe, and for my new plan to succeed.

Getting up from my bed, I went to look out my window. Street lights kept the darkness at bay, and I found that comforting now instead of annoying. I'd thought that light pollution was a nuisance when I'd tried to see the stars, but I was grateful for it now that I knew how scary the dark could be. I scanned the ground for monsters and was relieved when there were none. Hopefully, they were gone for good. Maybe Lucius had destroyed them all when he'd fought them the night I'd run from him.

Knowing that I needed my sleep so I could have enough energy to defeat him, I changed out of my clothes and into my nightgown. After setting my alarm, I lay down with the anticipation of a warrior who was going into battle the next day.

CHAPTER 21

I awoke with a bad feeling that was horribly familiar. It was the same feeling I'd had on the day Matt died. My heart pounding with dread, I braced myself to go see if Devon was alive.

But there was a knock on my door followed by my mom opening it without waiting for a response from me. "I heard your alarm go off, so I knew you were awake. How are you feeling?"

I forced a smile. "Good."

She beamed at me. "I got donuts to celebrate it being Friday. Come down and enjoy them with us."

That meant that my dad was already up too. With them knowing that I was awake, I couldn't take the chance of them finding me in a coma again. They would panic and take me to the hospital, and there'd be no way they'd let me go to Lucius's party tonight. I would lose my chance to save Devon in time.

If it wasn't already too late.

I couldn't go check, and my mind kept returning to how I'd denied him that kiss. What if that had been the last time I would ever see him?

No, I couldn't believe that. He was okay. He had to be.

I barely managed to eat one of my favorite donuts in the time my dad ate five. He mentioned my appointment with my new doctor next week, and I pretended to be on board with it.

"Is something wrong with your appetite?" Mom asked.

I thought fast. "No, but I'm kind of on a diet. Devon's party is tonight, and I want to look good."

"Oh, Hazel, you don't need to diet. You're a healthy weight, and you look beautiful."

"Thanks, Mom. It's not really about losing weight. I just don't want to look bloated."

"Are you dating this boy?" Dad asked sharply. "Because you said nothing about that when you introduced us to him."

I picked up my glass and took a sip of milk as I prepared my answer in my mind. "We weren't dating then, but we are now. This is our first date, actually."

I was using this as an opportunity to tell my parents about my relationship with Devon. If I defeated Lucius tonight and got Devon back, they would need to know that we were a couple.

"Your first date is at his birthday party?" Mom asked.

"Yeah," I said with a rueful smile. "And I'm meeting his dad. No pressure, right?"

I realized my mistake at her instantaneous worried expression. "You know you're not supposed to get stressed out. Maybe this isn't such a good idea."

"I was joking!" I exclaimed. Dialing down the desperation, I added, "I don't care what his dad thinks."

That was true, and my dad must have heard it in my voice. "You need to have respect for his father."

"No, I don't! I have respect for you, Dad, because you're a good dad. His father isn't. Do you know that this is the first birthday party Devon has had since he was thirteen? And that's only because he can walk now. Can you imagine how that must have made him feel? His dad sucks!"

Mom had tears in her eyes, and her hand was covering her mouth in distress. I knew that she was the one to make my plea to. "Please, Mom, Devon needs me there for moral support. And Abby is going with me."

"Abby? How is that a date?" Dad asked.

"Obviously, it's not like a normal date where we're going out alone. It's more like...we're presenting ourselves as a couple at his party. So, people will know we're together."

Dad seemed to like that idea. "I suppose it's fine if Abby and his father will be there. But I'd like you to invite him over again, so we can get to know him now that you're dating."

"I will," I said, hoping that I could keep that promise. I certainly wasn't going to invite Lucius to my house. I had to get Devon back, but the bad feeling wasn't going away.

"Go and be there for Devon," Mom said. "But come home if it gets too stressful. I'm sure he'll understand that you need to put your health first."

"Yes, absolutely," I agreed. "If anything goes wrong, I'll...come home."

The realization struck me while I was speaking. This might be the last conversation I ever had with my parents as myself. If Devon's theory was right, I could lose my memories again—this time permanently. I might not remember my parents at all. I might not know this love anymore.

Emotion choked me up, and I stood and walked around the table to them, reaching out my arms. Mom immediately got up and embraced me. I motioned my arm in a come-here gesture to my dad. Looking a bit confused, he came to join us in a group hug.

"I love you guys," I told them.

"Oh, sweet girl, we love you too," Mom said in a teary voice.

"We love you, Hazel," Dad said. "We're so glad you're okay."

That almost made me burst into tears, but I managed to get by with a few sniffles. "I'm so lucky to have such great parents."

I knew that now more than ever, and I didn't want to lose them. They would still be here for me if I forgot them, but it wouldn't be the same. All the precious memories I had of them would be gone. I didn't want that to happen.

But how could I leave Devon to die? I couldn't, no matter what happened to me.

The bad feeling was warning me about some kind of loss. I fervently hoped it wasn't about Devon. As much as I didn't want to lose my memories, losing him would be much worse. I would still lose him in a way, because I wouldn't remember him. I wouldn't have the memories of everything we'd shared. Him letting me ride his mom's horse, our kisses, our time together in the house, him telling me that he loved me. All gone.

But he'd be alive. It hurt to think of losing those memories, but it would hurt more to have them and lose him.

It was as I was saying goodbye to my parents and hoping it wasn't the last time I'd know them that the thought slithered in. What if I die instead of lose my memories?

My breath caught as I remembered that tragic day. The day Matt died. The day I would have died too if Devon hadn't driven me home.

Had the bad feeling been about Matt? Or had it been warning me that I was in danger?

Would this be my last time walking out of my house to go to school? Would it be my last day alive?

Of course it wouldn't, I told myself, but unease skittered down my spine. I jumped at the sudden sound of knocking behind me. Spinning around, I opened the front door to see Lucius standing there.

"What are you doing here?" I demanded.

"Hello, Devon," Dad said as he came up beside me. "I hear you're dating my daughter."

Lucius shot a surprised look toward me but recovered quickly, while I stood there mortified. "Yes sir, I am courting her."

"Courting?" Dad asked with a confused expression.

"It's an old-fashioned word for dating," Mom explained.

"More specifically, it means the man is wooing the woman with the intention of marriage," Lucius added.

"Marriage?" Dad said in alarm.

"I would of course, ask your permission first."

"You do that," Dad said dryly, watching him with a bemused expression.

"Uh, he's kidding," I said as I pushed open the screen door and forced Lucius to back up. "We're not getting married."

I turned to talk to my parents face to face. "I'm going straight to Abby's house after school. Her mom is going to drive us to the party."

I hadn't talked any of this over with Abby, but I couldn't deal with saying goodbye to my parents again. I needed to be strong and focused tonight, not an emotional mess.

Lucius's unexpected presence was a good distraction keeping me from dwelling on whether I would see my parents again. I still felt a pang when Mom told me to have a good day, and to call her if I needed her.

"I expect you to bring her home safe, Devon," Dad said, and my heart seized.

His gaze was fixed on Lucius as he continued. "I know you've got a lot to celebrate, but you will not drink and drive with my daughter in the car. Is that clear?"

"Abby's mom is—"

"I don't drive sir," Lucius interjected. He gestured toward his car. "My chauffeur is driving us."

Dad blinked. "What happened to your truck?"

A look of distaste crossed Lucius's face. "I wanted something more suitable."

I hoped that he hadn't gotten rid of Devon's truck, but that was the least of my worries right now. "Okay, we have to get to school. See you..."

I faltered on my usual parting words, because I didn't know if I would see them later. "Love you," I said and began to stride away so I wouldn't get emotional again.

"Wait!" Mom called after me. "You forgot your backpack."

I halted and turned back. She'd already gone and grabbed it for me by the time I walked back to the door. Handing it to me with an oblivious smile, she told me to have a good day.

"Thanks, you too," I said, trying to memorize her face so that the amnesia couldn't snatch it away from me.

With a sinking feeling, I realized that amnesia would be the best-case scenario out of the bad things that could happen. Because the other possibilities were me dying or Devon dying.

I cast a glowering look at Lucius as we started toward his car. I doubted I'd be having a bad feeling about his imminent death.

He raised his eyebrows at me. "Surely you don't prefer the truck."

"I prefer Devon," I snapped before immediately trying to appeal to any shred of humanity in him. Taking hold of his arm as I stopped and turned toward him, I said urgently, "Your world is falling apart without you. The ground is cracking open, and I don't know how much longer that house can stand. Devon's not safe there. You have to go back and save him."

He barked out a laugh and looked at me with real mirth in his eyes. "You want me to save him. How amusing."

"This is serious. He could die!"

His expression sobered. "And if the roles were reversed, would he save me?" he challenged.

My gaze dropped from his. "I would convince him to."

"Would you?" he asked with the note of challenge still in his voice.

My eyes met his again, and I spoke with sincerity. "Yes, Lucius. I want you to leave Devon's body, but I don't want you to *die*. You can live in your world, but he can't."

"Live?" he said derisively. "You think that's life? Being alone for years without a single soul for company, and following him around like a ghost while he squandered the life that should have been mine. I'm living it better than he ever could, so leave him to be put out of his misery and embrace your destiny with me."

"Never," I declared, dropping my hand from his arm. "I almost felt sorry for you until you started talking crap about him again. You know, we could all be friends if you weren't such an asshole to him. We could come to visit you now that we know how. That way you won't be lonely," I said, inspired enough by my solution to give him an excited smile.

He scowled at me, dashing my hopes.

"Is there a problem here?" my dad asked, and I turned at the sound of his voice to see him approaching us.

"No," I answered quickly. "Everything's fine." I couldn't let on that anything was wrong and give him a reason to prevent me from going to the party.

He eyed us suspiciously. "Aren't you supposed to be leaving for school?"

"Yes sir," Lucius said. "We were conversing and lost track of time."

Dad gave him an odd look, but I spoke up and drew his attention to me. "Yeah, we better get going. Thanks, Dad. Have a good day!"

Grabbing Lucius's arm, I tugged him away before he could use anymore words from a Jane Austin novel. "Talking," I muttered. "We say talking in this century."

He waved off the driver, who had started to get out of the car. Opening the door for me himself, Lucius waited for me to be seated before closing it and going around to the other side.

"You must read literature to appreciate the English language," he said as he sat down beside me.

I rolled my eyes. "You sound like Mr. Darcy."

"Ah, so you have read Pride and Prejudice."

"No, I just watched the movie."

His look of disappointment almost made me laugh, but the feeling of unease made it die in my throat. It was too similar to the feeling I'd had that day when tragedy had struck. The difference was that I hadn't known then that anything bad would happen, but now I did. Which was why I now felt dread in the pit of my stomach.

I fell silent and remained on edge the entire way to school, expecting us to be in a fatal accident at any moment. When we arrived safely, I stopped worrying about myself and went back to fearing for Devon.

It killed me to have to go to class instead of check on him, but I couldn't do anything that would end in a phone call to my parents. I considered trying to zap Lucius right there in the classroom, but it didn't seem like the right environment. There were too many authority figures who could intervene if it looked like something was wrong with me. I ran the risk of being sent to the hospital. That would delay things even more, and time was running out already.

And the party loomed large in my mind. My intuition was telling me that it would happen there.

But waiting was hard. The minutes ticked by at a torturously slow pace as I did little but watch the clock. Yet my building dread made the day go by too fast. I didn't want to find out what bad thing was about to happen.

My biggest fear was a repeat of what happened to Matt. Was I cursed to lose my boyfriends to tragic deaths? No, that couldn't happen to me again! I hadn't been able to save Matt, but I would save Devon.

Even if it meant losing my memory or my life in the process. A big part of me found it impossible to accept the idea that I might die. Trying to imagine not being alive was surreal. I thought about Svetlana and wondered if I'd be a ghost. But she'd only been one until her body was discovered. My body would be...

I shuddered at the thought of being buried and banished those morbid thoughts from my mind. I needed to be mentally strong and focused on defeating Lucius.

CHAPTER 22

"This is a bad idea," Abby said as we stepped off the school bus. Lucius had offered me a ride home, but I'd declined and told him I'd see him at the party.

"I'll send the car for you," he'd said.

"No, thanks. Abby's mom will drive us."

Something had flickered in his eyes before he'd continued in a brisk tone. "No need to trouble her mother. My driver will collect you both."

He had stridden away before I could refuse, but I'd shrugged it off. He probably didn't know Abby's address anyway. I didn't bother mentioning it to her as we took the bus to her street.

I hadn't told her about my bad feeling either, but it sounded like she wanted to back out of the plan anyway.

"I mean doing it at his party," she said as I shot her a sideways look. "You should wait until—"

"I can't wait," I cut in and told her about visiting Devon and how the ground was literally crumbling around him.

"We think it's because Lucius left," I explained as we approached her house.

I shared our theory with her, and my worries that Devon couldn't survive there much longer. "I have to do it tonight before it's too late."

"Talk to Lucius," she suggested. "I bet he doesn't know what's happening there. If you tell him that Devon—"

"He knows. I told him this morning, and he didn't care."

She stared at me, her gaze flattening as it went from shocked to bleak. "So, he really is a bad guy."

"Yeah," I said with a sigh. "I even told him that we can all be friends and visit him there so he won't be lonely, but he didn't want that."

Her derisive laugh surprised me. "Of course, he doesn't want to be friends with you when he wants to be with you."

I blinked at her. "What? No, he doesn't."

"He told me himself that you're his perfect match."

I scoffed. "Well, I'm *not*. He thinks he can just replace Devon and make me forget all about him, but that's never going to happen."

Realizing what I'd just said, I winced and added, "Hopefully."

She came to a standstill and turned to face me. "What do you mean hopefully? Does he have some kind of forgetting spell?"

"Not exactly," I responded ruefully. "Let's go inside, and I'll explain."

Her disapproving look didn't bode well for her still being on board with my plan after hearing the risks. I'd thought about not telling her, but I couldn't let her be blindsided by something bad happening to me.

She plopped down on her couch and crossed her arms. "Tell me," she commanded.

I remained standing and tried to downplay my words even as I spoke them. "Um, well, Devon thinks that maybe I might get amnesia again if I do this. But he's probably wrong. The doctor said it was stress, so..."

Her eyes narrowed, and she uncrossed her arms to point a finger at me. "You think Devon is right. That's why you're telling me about this, so I can be prepared. Are you kidding me, Hazel? I can't let you do this!"

"And I can't let Devon die!"

Her face fell, and she slumped in defeat. I sat down next to her and tried to comfort her. "I might be fine. We could be worrying about nothing."

There was no way I could tell her about the even worse possibility of my death if she was taking this so hard. I also decided not to mention that the amnesia might be permanent.

But she came to that conclusion on her own. "He thinks you won't get your memory back this time. That's why it's such a big deal."

I sprang up and started pacing. "He doesn't know for sure. It's not like he's some expert on all this stuff. So much for looking like a warlock."

My bitterness came out in my tone, because I was upset with him for refusing to help me save him. He was willing to die to protect me, which sounded romantic. But it would mean that I would lose him, and that would be the end of our romance. In his mind, so would me forgetting him. But we could fall in love again if he was alive. I had still been drawn to him when I hadn't remembered him.

"Did you tell Lucius about this?" Abby asked.

I shot her a sharp look. "When you're planning a sneak attack on someone, telling him about it takes away the element of surprise. So no, I didn't."

"But maybe if he knew you might lose your memory, he would—"

"He wants me to forget Devon, remember?"

Her shoulders slumped again. "Right, so you can be with him instead."

"That'll never happen."

"But if you lose your memory, it could. You're attracted to Devon, and he looks exactly like him."

I shook my head. "No, because I didn't feel that for him when I had amnesia. There's something more with Devon. Something that's always pulled me toward him right from the start."

"What is it?" she asked intently. "What's been pulling you toward him?"

Her keen interest made me want to give her more than a one-word answer. "I called it love at first sight, but how can you love someone you don't know? But Lucius proved that it was more than Devon's looks, or I would have had the same reaction to him."

She nodded, hanging on my every word.

"So, after everything that's happened, I think it was destiny."

Abby recoiled from that answer. "He is not my destiny."

"What?" I asked, confused. "Who?"

She scrambled to her feet. "I mean your destiny. You don't know if he's your destiny. You're still in high school."

I recalled her commenting that I might marry Matt someday, but it felt wrong to bring that up, so I went with something lighter. "I'm not that girl at the coffee shop. You don't have to motivate me to get good grades."

Although I hadn't paid attention in any of my classes since I'd returned to school. If I didn't fix this mess soon, I probably *would* fail.

"Oh," she said with a flustered laugh. "Right. Um, anyway, I'm going to take a shower. Or, did you want to take one first?"

I scoffed. "I'm not taking a shower. If I stink, too bad. Lucius can deal with it."

"You don't stink," she assured me.

"Neither do you. Just relax. Let's watch a fun, girly movie before we go. You pick."

She smiled, but it was a weak smile. "Put on whatever you want. I'm just gonna take a quick shower."

I sighed as she went upstairs. I hadn't expected her to be intimidated by wealth, but she was obviously nervous about going to this party. If it wasn't for this bad feeling, I would have been impatient to get there and finish this. As it was, I couldn't focus on a movie either, so I went up to wait for Abby in her room.

That's when I saw the prom dress hanging on her open closet door. It was dark blue, long, and had an overlay of tulle. Surely, she wasn't going to wear it to the party.

"When did you buy this?" I asked her when she walked in quite a bit later with her hair curled. I'd wondered what she'd been doing in there for all that time after I heard the shower stop. Now I knew she'd been using the curling iron.

"Yesterday after I left your house," she replied. "My mom went with me. I'm sorry I didn't ask you to go, but I knew you wanted to see Devon."

"No, you were right. I needed to go see him."

I almost added that I wouldn't have wasted a penny on trying to look good for Lucius's party, but that would be kind of mean since she'd already bought the dress. "This is beautiful," I said instead.

Her dreamy smile made me glad I hadn't spoiled the moment. "I feel like a princess in it."

I smiled as I imagined us getting ready for prom months from now.

"What are you going to wear?"

"To prom?" I asked, wondering if I'd spoken my thoughts aloud.

"Um, to the party," she said, looking at me like I needed mental help.

"Oh, uh, this," I said, spreading out my arms and showing her the clothes I had on. Which were the same ones I'd worn to school.

She gave me a deadpan look. "You know you're going to be meeting Devon's dad."

That gave me a momentary pause, but I shook it off. "I don't care about impressing him. He sucks."

"But Devon still has to live with him. He could decide not to let him date you if you don't get on his good side."

I snorted. "Devon wouldn't listen to him. He does what he wants to do."

She shrugged. "Okay." Brightening as she changed the subject, she said, "I wonder what kind of food they'll have. I can't believe we're going to a dinner party in a mansion!"

Just like her enthusiasm over Lucius's castle, this was a side to Abby I hadn't seen before. Thinking back on it, I guess I had when we were kids. I'd shared in it back then when we'd imagined ourselves as princesses. But I'd grown out of that, while she apparently had held on to her childish excitement over such things.

I wouldn't ruin it for her by reminding her of the real reason I was going. I'd mentioned some of the risks to her so she wouldn't be blind-sided, and I didn't need to keep stressing her out with them. Maybe she wanted to escape from thinking about that and pretend like we were going to some fairytale ball.

She certainly looked the part when she put on her elegant, A-line off the shoulder dress. The tulle gave it structure, on it was long and full like Cinderella's gown. But it was a dark blue, so it didn't match Abby's sky-blue eyes. She was stunning nonetheless, and a bit sexy with her blonde hair in loose curls rather than upswept.

Her mom gushed over how beautiful she was and took pictures of us. I felt a bit self-conscious standing next to Abby in my jeans and t-shirt, but I decided to just go with it. This was her night to shine, and I celebrated it with her. Taking the phone from her mom, I urged her parents to pose with Abby for a family photo. It was a great picture, with all three of them smiling happily.

The doorbell rang, and Abby's dad went to answer it. He came back with a perplexed look on his face. "Did you order an Uber? There's a guy outside claiming to be your driver."

"Are you kidding me?" I exclaimed. "He sent his driver here? How'd he know your address?"

"Who did?" Abby's dad asked.

"Lu—"

Abby spoke over me quickly. "Devon! It was Devon. He sent his driver to pick us up."

"Right," I confirmed. "He said he was going to do that."

"How nice," Abby's mom said. "That's so thoughtful of him."

Abby's dad didn't trust as easily as her mom. "Maybe I should drive you."

"No, Dad, he's already here. That would be rude."

"Yeah," I agreed, not wanting him anywhere near Lucius with his cop instincts. I doubted he would know he wasn't really Devon, but it was better not to take the chance of arousing his suspicions. "He's driven me to school before, if that's what you're worried about. He's a good driver."

"You've seen him before? Come and identify him."

Abby rolled her eyes, but I followed her dad to the door and looked at the driver on the doorstep. "That's him. We're okay."

But my bad feeling intensified as we stepped outside.

CHAPTER 23

t was worse than this morning, because Abby was now with me. What if we got into an accident on the way to the party? What if she was injured? Devon's accident popped into my head, and how he'd ended up paralyzed. What if that happened to Abby? What if I died and couldn't be here for her?

My apprehension grew with every street we turned onto, expecting it to be the one we would crash on. I braced myself for a collision with another car. Maybe a drunk driver like the one who had killed Matt. Or someone racing down the road to evade the police.

I should have been relieved when we made it unharmed to Devon's house, but I stared at it with dread. That was where it would happen. I knew it without knowing what it was.

Stepping out of the car and closing the distance to the door felt like I was walking to my execution. So maybe I really would die. I tried to muster the courage I'd had when I'd thrown myself in front of Devon, but it wasn't so easy to face death when you had time to think about it. Everything had happened so fast before, but this was being drawn out too much. I needed to get it over with.

But Lucius didn't even look at me when he opened the door. We hadn't knocked, so his driver must have alerted him of our arrival. I rolled my eyes when I saw that he was wearing a tuxedo, but his eyes were riveted on Abby.

"Milady," he said. "You are luminous."

She really was with her blonde hair and blue eyes, but it was more than that. She had a glow tonight that radiated from her. Maybe it was her excitement about this party, and the smile that lit up her face at his awestruck words.

Oh no.

I saw the way she was gazing back at him, and my heart sank. I'd wanted this for her, but not with him. He was the enemy.

But he appeared to be just as smitten with her as he stood there transfixed.

"Thank you," Abby replied. "You look...really good too."

She blushed and stumbled on. "Uh, thanks for inviting us. And for sending your driver to bring us here."

That was when he remembered that I was there too. His gaze shifted to me and instantly cooled. "Come in, Hazel. I will introduce you to my father."

He made it sound like he was only inviting me in, and I glanced at Abby to see her embarrassed expression, which she quickly covered up with a blank mask that didn't fool me.

I turned my attention back to Lucius and glared at him. "*We* will meet your father." I swept my arm and urged, "C'mon, Abby. Ladies first."

I'd hoped that my quip would lighten her mood, but she didn't crack a smile as she stiffly stepped inside. I followed her and scowled at Lucius when he offered me his arm. Moving to stand beside Abby, I made an imperious gesture with my hand. "Lead the way."

Annoyance flashed across his face, but he did as I commanded and walked alone in front of us as we followed him together. I shot a look at Abby to see how she was doing, and she was glancing around, taking it all in. Any other time, I would have been doing the same, but I was too upset and worried to notice much other than it was a modern mansion. I briefly wondered what it had looked like before Devon's dad remodeled it, when it had historic charm.

Then we entered a room that did catch my attention. It was a bar with a bartender stationed behind it like at a real establishment. A pool table stood on the other side of the large room, while this side held leather chairs and a glass-topped coffee table. There was also a couch facing a very modern fireplace that I thought might be just for show.

Lucius led us to the men seated in the chairs by the coffee table, and I knew immediately which one was Devon's dad. The resemblance was unmistakable, although his eyes were blue. He was still an extremely handsome man, made even more so when he smiled at Lucius.

Lucius took my hand, and I didn't jerk it out of his grasp like I wanted to. "Father, I present to you my beloved, Hazel."

I had to play my part, even as anger churned in my gut. He'd been looking at my best friend like she was the girl for him, and now I was his beloved? Why was he leading her on and then giving her the cold shoulder? How dare he mess with her feelings like that!

Not that I wanted her with him, but I still wanted to kick him in the balls for how he was ignoring her right now. His dad's smile slipped as he assessed my appearance, and I took satisfaction in it, even though I shouldn't. As Abby had said, this man had control over Devon's life. I should be trying to win him over, but I didn't have it in me.

"Nice to meet you, Mr. Culver. It's so great of you to have a belated birthday party for Devon."

His gaze turned icy, probably because he picked up on the criticism in my fake compliment. "Yes, and we have much to celebrate with his miraculous recovery. And now he has you too."

I wasn't going to let that dig go. "I was here *before*. I just missed out on the pleasure of meeting you," I said with the most obvious false sweetness ever.

His eyes narrowed at me as one of his friends cleared his throat. The noise shifted his gaze from me, and he saw Abby, who was hanging back a little way from us. His eyes warmed with approval. "And who is this lovely young lady?"

Using it as the perfect excuse to remove my hand from Lucius's hold, I stepped back and pulled Abby forward. "This is Abby, my best friend."

Mr. Culver stood and extended his hand to her. "It's a pleasure to meet you, Abby."

As she shook his hand, he shot Lucius a look that clearly questioned why he hadn't chosen her instead of me. I was wondering that myself.

He had no reason to want me to be his girlfriend when he was attracted to Abby.

Was it just to spite Devon? It wasn't enough for him to steal his body and his life. He had to steal his girlfriend too?

Well, he had no chance in hell of doing that. I was sending him back to where he came from, and the increasingly bad feeling was warning me that I'd better do it soon. Probably not in front of Devon's dad though. As much as I disliked him, he didn't need to see his son collapse in front of him.

That thought made me realize that it would be best if Lucius was sitting down when I zapped him with my power. I didn't want him to hit Devon's head on the floor if I dropped him from a standing position.

So, I forced myself to wait until we were seated for dinner. In the meantime, I tried to gather my inner strength as we left the bar and went to mingle with the arriving guests. Lucius had apparently ensured that Abby and I arrived before everyone else. We knew some of the other people from school, but none of them were our friends. They were all the popular kids, and they were thrilled to be invited to what would normally be a boring party for them. There was no drinking and no loud music.

But there was a mansion, and they were not from wealthy families, so they were impressed. There were also rich kids here who attended the private school that Devon's dad wanted him to go to now that he wanted to show him off to everyone.

Lucius was doing the same thing to me as people sought his attention. "Girlfriend," I snapped at him, uncaring that the girls he'd just introduced me to heard me. "It's girlfriend, not beloved. Talk like a normal person."

"I think it's romantic," one of the girls gushed.

"It is," the other one agreed. "You're so lucky to have a boyfriend who cares about romance."

"Yes, so lucky," I said. "Excuse me. I have to go to the bathroom."

I turned to get Abby, who was again hanging back from us. To my pleasant surprise, I saw that she was talking to a cute guy. He wasn't someone I recognized, so he must go to private school. With my first real smile of the evening, I walked off to take a break from this party.

As I stepped out into the hallway, I said, "Be ready, Devon. I'll do it during dinner. Get back in there as soon as he—"

The force of the feeling cut off my words. This wasn't just foreboding and dread; it was terrifying certainty. The bad thing was happening now. I spun around and ran back, my feet taking me toward the horror instead of away from it.

Everything looked normal as I charged into the room, but then I spotted them. Lucius and Abby in some kind of confrontation as the guy she had been talking to watched them. In that instant, I knew. It wasn't me or Devon. It was Abby who was in danger.

My heart thudded in panic as Lucius reached for her arm. Was he going to hurt her? The short distance was too far for me to stop him, but he stilled instead of pulling her away, as it looked like he'd been about to do. A stricken look came over his face as I made it to them.

Fresh terror came over me as I realized he'd seen something. He had the same ability as Devon. He'd touched her and seen something bad.

Abby didn't know, because she was still glaring at him. Only seconds had passed as I grabbed my phone, but it was too long. It was too late. Both the anguish in Lucius's eyes and my overwhelming sense of doom told me that. I tapped in 911 anyway.

"Picture the castle," Lucius told Abby in desperation. "Imagine yourself there."

"What?" Abby asked, looking bewildered now.

"Yes, do it!" I urged, grasping onto his idea. "Hello, I need an ambulance."

"Hazel, what are you doing?" Abby questioned.

"Imagine yourself at the castle," I called to her. "Please!"

Lucius held onto her with an intense look of concentration, and I sensed that he was trying to give her some of his power. Of course! Because she didn't have the spell right now.

Shoving my phone at the guy she'd been talking to, I said, "Tell them the address, and to hurry."

Taking hold of Abby's other arm, I pleaded, "Focus on the castle."

I saw her nod as I focused on giving her some of my power too.

Then she collapsed.

Stunned despite knowing it was coming, I reacted slower than Lucius. He caught her before I even shot out my other hand to reach for her. People gasped and cried out, and I heard the guy urgently speaking into my phone.

Lucius sank down onto the floor, being careful to gently lower Abby with him and cradle her head on his lap. He gave me a grim look. "I shall see if she's there."

He closed his eyes and slumped over her.

His head was lifting before I could react, and he blinked like he was disoriented. When his dark eyes focused on me, I knew.

"Devon!" I exclaimed.

He gazed at me in amazement. "I'm back."

"You are," I said, a smile breaking over my face, but it was quickly stolen by worry for Abby.

Devon looked down at her too and felt her wrist for a pulse. When he raised his head, he had the bleakest expression I'd ever seen. But he called out, "Does anyone know CPR?"

"I do," the guy said, handing me back my phone. "The ambulance is on the way."

He moved Abby onto the floor and knelt beside her. Leaning down, he began to alternate between chest compressions and blowing air into her mouth.

I watched, trying to ignore the hollow feeling inside me as I held onto futile hope. A fantasy played out in my mind of this guy saving Abby. He was her hero, and he came to visit her in the hospital. They started dating when she got out. He took her to prom, and she wore this dress in honor of the day they met, and when he saved her life.

"Let us through please."

I blinked back to reality and stepped out of the way of the paramedics. Abby's guy rose to his feet and let them take over.

The nightmare was still happening. Abby wasn't at prom having a lovely time with her heroic guy. She was unmoving and unresponsive on the floor.

She was in a coma, I told myself. Just like I had been. She was in Lucius's world, but she would return and be fine.

The look that passed between the paramedics confirmed my worst fears. "Are her parents here?" one of them asked.

"I'll call them," I said, numbness spreading over me.

He rattled off the name of the hospital they were taking her to as they loaded her onto a stretcher and rushed her out to the ambulance.

I called Abby's house and robotically relayed the information to her mom when she answered. Everything felt unreal and distant.

My eyes fell on Devon, and he stared back at me with haunted eyes. He knew it too. Of course he did, because he'd had contact with her when he came back. His ability had told him what I didn't want to accept.

Abby was dead.

CHAPTER 24

"What are you doing on the floor?" Mr. Culver demanded. "Get up."

Devon tried to push himself up on his arms and stand, but his legs didn't move. "I can't."

"Of course you can," his father insisted. "Get up this instant."

Something in me snapped. "Abby was taken away in an ambulance! Do you care about that?"

He turned his attention to me. "I was just notified of it. You said it was Abby? The young woman in the blue dress? What happened?"

"She fainted. I did CPR, but she was still unconscious when the paramedics got here. I think..."

Abby's would-be savior trailed off, his expression bleak. "I hope she's gonna be okay."

"Of course she will," Mr. Culver said. "She's a healthy young woman." His gaze hardened as it landed back on Devon. "And you're a healthy young man. Get up."

Devon ignored him and spoke to me. "Go. Don't wait for me. I'll be there as soon as I can."

"But," I began, torn between needing to get to the hospital and not wanting to leave him in this situation.

"Our driver will take you," he said and dug in his pockets. "Damn it! I don't have my phone." He fixed a hard look on his father. "Hazel needs a ride to the hospital immediately."

"Of course," he said, pulling out his phone and making a quick call. "He'll meet you outside," he told me, probably all too happy to get rid of me.

"Thanks." My gaze flitted to Devon, and he jerked his chin in a gesture for me to go.

I turned and walked out of there, hearing Devon say that he needed his wheelchair.

"The hell you do! Your legs work just fine now. Stop playing games and get up. What, are you mad I didn't like your girlfriend? Date her if you want to for all I care. You'll tire of her soon enough and…"

His father's voice faded as I got further down the hall. I focused on the door ahead of me like it was my only hope. Once I got outside, I'd be away from this cursed place. Then everything would be restored to the way it was before. I'd get to the hospital and discover that Abby had been revived. It would all be okay just like it was last time.

My bad feeling was gone now, so I was able to convince myself that my wishful thinking was true. Bursting out from the oppressive atmosphere inside the house and breathing in the evening air helped too.

But sitting in the back of the car with only the silent driver for company brought back my anxiety. It felt like we should be speeding to the hospital instead of driving at a normal pace. But that wasn't necessary, because the ambulance had already done that. The emergency had passed, and Abby was safely at the hospital. Everything was okay now.

Pulling out my phone, I called my mom. "Can you meet me at the hospital? Abby's there again."

I was surprised at how shaky and scared my voice sounded. Yes, I'd had a scare, but there was nothing to fear anymore. Devon was back, and Abby was getting the medical care she needed. She'd be fine, and this would all seem like a bad dream.

I probably wouldn't be allowed in to see her tonight, but that was okay. Another thought occurred to me. She might be in surgery. I remembered her telling me that she might need it if the medicine didn't work. Which it obviously hadn't since she'd collapsed again.

"Hazel, calm down," Mom said as I took a breath after babbling all of that to her. "We're on our way."

"Thanks, Mom. Maybe you should take two cars, so you can go home if she's in surgery. I want to wait there until it's done."

"We'll wait with you," she said.

When I arrived at the hospital, it was all wrong. I'd expected the staff not to give us any information, but Abby's parents didn't come out to tell us anything either. We were told to wait for notification from the family.

"But where are they?" I demanded. "I need to talk to them. Abby's my best friend, and I was with her when the ambulance came for her."

"They're probably waiting with her before surgery," Mom said, tugging me away from the reception desk. "It takes time to prep for it."

"But if it was an emergency, shouldn't she be in surgery already?"

"We can't make any assumptions," Dad said. "They'll let us know when they can. Their daughter is their priority, and we have to be patient and wait."

So, we sat there as time ticked by and people trickled in to the emergency room for treatment. I watched the doors like a hawk, anticipating seeing Abby's parents coming out to tell us that she was okay.

But when they finally appeared, I knew that she wasn't. Abby's stepfather had his arm around her mom, trying to comfort her, but tears were streaming down his face too. My mom cried out at the sight of them and rushed over.

"Oh shit," my dad said, getting up to follow her.

I stayed seated, burning with a steadily building anger as the adults were overcome by grief. It wasn't going to end this way. My best friend wasn't going to die.

She better be there. It was the last thought I had as I pictured the castle.

I ended up at Lucius's stupid wall of fog, along with a swarm of monsters. Sending out my power in a blaze of fury, I torched them with a look. They turned to ashes within seconds.

"Impressive."

I whirled to see Lucius standing there in his demon form, still dressed in the tuxedo he'd worn to the party. "Where's Abby?"

"Inside." He gestured for me to walk through the wall.

I hurried forward and entered the fog, rushing toward the castle. Lucius caught up to me and strode beside me, now looking human.

"She'll be glad to see you. She's having a difficult time accepting her death."

I halted and spun to shove him. "She is not dead!"

He righted himself and gave me a pained look. "She told me herself that the doctor pronounced her dead. She's able to see everything happening at the hospital, and it's upsetting her. You need to convince her to keep her focus here. She won't listen to me."

"Of course it's upsetting her! Why aren't you helping her get back to her body?"

His gaze hardened, and he looked at me with grave severity. "Her body is deceased. She cannot live in it. I thought you understood that when you urged her to escape to this world. You knew death was coming for her."

"I was..."

I faltered, because he was right. I *had* known that she was in serious danger, and that the only way to save her was to send her here. But I hadn't thought beyond that.

She had been dying in that moment, but I hadn't considered her actually being dead. It had seemed like a temporary solution until she got to the hospital where the doctors would bring her back from the brink of death.

Except they hadn't.

I stared at Lucius in disbelief. "She's dead?"

"In your world. She's alive here."

This was too confusing, and I wasn't going to waste any more time trying to understand it. I just wanted to see Abby. Without another word to him, I pivoted and continued to the castle. He got ahead of me and opened the door.

I rushed past him and yelled, "Abby! Abby, where are you?"

"She's in the dining hall. There's no need for shouting." Taking long strides, he led the way.

Abby looked up when we entered the room, and she sprang from her chair to run to me. "Hazel!"

We both burst into tears as we threw our arms around each other. "I was so scared for you," I cried.

"I saw you at the hospital. And my parents. It was so horrible for them when the doctor told them. And when they were saying goodbye to me. They couldn't see that I was right there with them, and they couldn't hear me. They are so sad, Hazel. I've never seen my dad cry before. God, it broke my heart."

She sobbed and hugged me tighter. I desperately tried to think of a way to fix this, but I was starting to realize that this was much different than being in a coma. Abby couldn't just get back inside her body, or she would have done it when she'd been there with her parents. I knew how natural and instinctive it was, because that was where we belonged.

Until...

Abby came to the same realization as she cried herself out and pulled back to look at me. "I'm really dead. Like, for real."

I didn't want to confirm that. "There has to be a way to bring you back. A spell maybe." I brightened with that thought.

"There isn't."

I whirled on Lucius. "How do you know? And this is all your fault anyway. If it hadn't been for you, she'd be—"

"In heaven instead of here. If you believe in that sort of thing."

I stared at him. "No, she'd be..."

"Oh, so you don't believe. Then why did you think the exorcism would work?"

"I do believe, but Abby wouldn't be...dead." Even as I said it, I realized that I was wrong.

"Really?" he challenged. "The paramedics weren't able to revive her. She was already dead before they transported her to the hospital."

"They kept trying anyway," Abby said. "They didn't give up the whole way there, and the one kept saying c'mon kid. But when we got there, they said I'd had no pulse when they arrived on scene, and that they hadn't been able to restart my heart at all."

She looked at me with haunted eyes. "I died at the party."

Glancing down at herself, she added, "At least I was wearing something pretty. If I'm going to be stuck in one outfit for eternity, this is the best one. None of my other clothes compare to this."

"There are numerous gowns here at your disposal. Perhaps Hazel will use her magic to transform them into the colors of your choosing before she leaves."

I scowled at him. "I'm not leaving her here."

"Oh?" he enquired, casually crossing his arms and raising his eyebrows. "Are you staying here with us?"

"You can't," Abby said. "Your parents are freaking out. They think you fainted because of me, but they'll really lose it if they realize you're in a coma again. You've gotta go back now!"

"You can see that? How? You've been standing here with us the whole time I've been here."

She shrugged. "It's kind of like a window into the hospital. If I focus on it, I can see what's happening there."

I watched her eyes go distant, and then her gaze cleared and fixed on me. "Yeah, your dad is yelling for someone to help you, and your mom is falling apart. You can't do this to them. Please go back."

She looked so sad as she added, "It's bad enough that my parents are suffering. Don't make yours suffer too."

"But what about you?" I asked. I didn't want to hurt my parents, but Abby was hurting too. She needed me to help her through this.

"I'll be okay. Maybe you can come back tomorrow night after your parents are asleep," she said in a hopeful tone.

"Or tonight after we get home." I paused there with a pang of realization that she couldn't go home. Maybe never again. No, I couldn't accept that. There had to be a way.

"No, don't risk it," she cautioned me. "They might check on you to make sure you're okay. You better wait until tomorrow."

"Okay," I agreed reluctantly. Moving in to give her a hug, I said, "Don't worry. I'll figure out a way to get you out of here."

"Thanks, Hazel," she replied. But her sad smile as she pulled away from me revealed that she didn't believe that would happen.

My gaze shifted to Lucius, and I skewered him with a glare. "Find a spell."

He shook his head. "You're talking about necromancy. I have no spells for raising the dead; nor do I know if such spells exist."

"Nope," Abby said. "Remember Pet Cemetery? You're not doing that to me, Hazel. I'm not coming back as some evil thing that's going to murder my parents. Promise me that you won't mess around with anything like that."

I waved my hand dismissively. "That was a movie. Jesus brought people back to life, and they weren't evil."

"You're not Jesus. Promise me, Hazel," she insisted, grabbing onto my arm and giving me an intense look. "Promise me that you won't do any spells to bring me back."

I didn't want to be bound by that promise. "But what if—"

"Promise me!" she demanded, cutting me off.

"I promise," I said, deflating with defeat.

"It'll be okay," she assured me, even though we both knew it wasn't.

I'd gotten Devon back but lost my best friend. It was too heavy of a price to pay. I was the one who was supposed to be in danger, not Abby. This was my fight, not hers.

I glowered at Lucius, but it was weak. I hadn't beaten him. He'd only left Devon's body out of concern for Abby. He'd known that she'd be here by herself without him, and he'd cared enough to jeopardize his victory over Devon in order to ensure that she wasn't alone.

Did he know that Devon had reclaimed his body? I couldn't tell from his flat stare. "Go back," he said. "You got what you wanted, so go and be happy with him."

My anger sparked again. "This isn't what I wanted! How can I be happy without Abby? Why would you even think that?"

"You have your precious Devon," he said, coldly twisting the knife. "Enjoy your reunion."

"Hazel," Abby interjected. "You need to go now. It's getting bad at the hospital."

"Damn it! I'll be back tomorrow," I promised her and blinked back into my body.

CHAPTER 25

Chaos surrounded me as I opened my eyes. I was being rushed down a hallway on a wheeled stretcher while my mom sobbed and pleaded, "Please save her."

"She's unconscious," my dad said. "She's not..."

"We'll take care of her," a male voice said. "Please don't—"

"Mom?" I said, feeling disoriented. "Dad? I'm okay."

The stretcher came to a blessed stop, allowing me to focus, even with my mom's startled screech. "Hazel! You're awake!"

I sat up. "Yeah, I'm sorry."

"Take it easy," the orderly said, gently pushing my shoulder in an attempt to get me to lay back down.

"Yes," my dad agreed. "You've had a big shock. You need to be checked out."

Evading the orderly, I swung my legs and hopped off the stretcher. "I'm fine. See? Let's go home."

Unfortunately, declaring myself okay didn't convince my parents. I had to wait for a doctor to tell them the same thing after examining me, which took another hour. We were all exhausted by then, but we were also avoiding what had caused me to pass out. None of us mentioned Abby.

So, when I woke up in my bed the next morning, it all just seemed like a bad dream. I even grabbed my phone off my nightstand to text her, but my fingers paused over the keyboard.

There was a text from Devon that I had ignored, but I had seen part of it. I'm so sorry. Call me when

I went back to it and braced myself to tap on it. There wasn't much more to it beyond telling me to call him when I could and letting him know if there was anything he could do. It confirmed what I knew deep down inside. Last night had been real, and Abby was dead.

Kind of.

It was a weird situation, and it was what held me together. She wasn't completely out of reach like she would have been if she wasn't in Lucius's world. That made it seem not as final—like it could be reversed. But Abby had made me promise not to try.

An idea formed in my mind as I looked at Devon's text. He hadn't been part of that promise. He could work some magic to bring her back.

"No," he flat out refused after I called him and suggested it. "I'm not doing that. Don't even ask me to."

"But you asked if there was anything you could do to help, and this is what you can do."

"I don't know of any spell that can bring someone back to life, but I wouldn't try it even if I did. You know what happened the last time I messed around with magic. It went very wrong, and I created a monster."

A chill ran through me as Abby's words about turning into an evil entity came back to me. "But we can't just leave her there."

"Is it still falling apart?"

"No," I said with a dawning realization. "It was normal. At least by the castle. I didn't go look by the house. I'll check when I go back tonight."

He expelled a breath. "Damn that asshole. He's ruining everything again. If he would have left her alone, she would have moved on like she was supposed to. Instead, he's using her to reel you back in. Don't let him, Hazel. I know it's hard, but you need to let her go and cut him out of your life."

I processed what he was saying in disbelief, and then anger. "Moved on? You mean died. You're saying she should have died instead of escaping to his world."

"She did die! She's not in a coma, Hazel. She's dead. She can't come back here, and now she's stuck there. This is so messed up."

I was starting to get his point, and it took the fight out of me. I'd been so sure when I'd urged Abby to leave her body and go to the castle, but had it been the right thing to do? But how could I have let her die? I'd known instinctively that it was her only chance for survival.

Had that been the wrong decision? I'd been so happy to see her, but she'd been so sad. I thought about Svetlana, and how I'd helped her spirit move on. Had I done the opposite to Abby? Had I kept her lingering instead of letting her go?

But Abby wasn't a ghost. "She's alive there."

"And now he's using her to lure you there. How long will it be before he traps you?"

"He can't. I know how to use my power now. I burned up those monsters we were so scared of."

"Burned them? How?"

"I don't even know, actually. I was really mad and blasted my power at them, and they were instantly on fire. Too bad we didn't know to do that before. Who knows what else we can do."

"You're saying we like I had anything to do with it. You're the one who has this power, not me."

"I think you do too. And if we combine our power, we might be able to get Abby back. If we go to the hospital right now and find her—"

"No," he cut in. "I told you I'm not doing a spell like that."

"It's not a spell. I don't even have a spell. It's just you and me sending our power to her body."

"To make a zombie?"

"Devon! No, to heal her. Wait, maybe we can use the healing spell! Why didn't I think of that last night? Damn it! But everything happened so fast."

"You can't heal a dead body."

"How do you know when we haven't tried?"

He sighed. "You're in denial, and that's a normal stage of grief. You'd be able to get past it if that asshole hadn't interfered. It's all messed up now, and I don't see a way to fix it."

"I'm telling you the way. Meet me at the hospital, and we can at least try."

"They wouldn't let us see the body anyway. Only her parents would be allowed to do that, and we're not putting them through that."

Abby had told me how hard that had been for them, and I didn't want to cause them anymore pain. If only there was a way that I could make them understand...

"Yeah, you're right. Okay, I have to go now. I'll talk to you later."

"Hazel," he said suspiciously, "what are you—"

"Bye!" I said quickly and ended the call.

Getting dressed in a hurry, I folded a piece of notebook paper and shoved it in my pocket. Putting a pen in my other pocket, I lay down in bed and pictured the house in Lucius's world. Instantly, I was there.

I gaped in astonishment, because the huge hole in the yard was gone. It looked exactly as it had when I first wandered across it, with unbroken ground and dry, yellow grass. Even more astounding was that the trees stood where they previously had, like they had never fallen. I glanced up at the bleak but calm sky. No unnatural lightning and booming thunder. Everything had been restored to how it had been before.

Because Lucius had returned. Had he done some sort of magic to set it all back to how he'd had it, or had it happened automatically because of his presence? Had his world mended itself upon his return as it had begun falling apart when he'd left?

I had no time to ponder it all now, so I jogged up the porch steps and entered the house. The spell I needed sat open on the coffee table, which led me to believe that Devon had been trying to use it to get back to his body. I couldn't imagine how scared he must have been, probably imagining this house being swallowed up into that approaching hole at any second.

It was such a relief to know that he was safe at home. If only Abby was too.

I almost grabbed the paper with the spell on it, but I decided to copy it instead. It was best to leave it here in case I ever needed it again—for someone else. All I had to do was picture my room, and I was back there.

It was a shame that I hadn't had time to visit with Abby, but I was on a mission. Of course, I couldn't tell my parents about it, so I had to sit through breakfast first. Smelling the food triggered my hunger, and I ate more than I had expected to.

"That was really good," I said and then noticed my parents giving me odd looks.

"I'm glad you've got your appetite," Mom said.

And I realized how weird it was for me to be enjoying my food when my best friend was dead. "Uh, I didn't get to eat dinner yesterday, because of what happened."

It made me sad that Abby hadn't gotten to eat that fancy meal she had been looking forward to. There had been silver covered dishes set out before her at the castle, but she hadn't been eating when I arrived. I hoped she'd had something after I left.

"Oh, I didn't even think of that," Mom fretted. "You should have told me you wanted something. We could have stopped at a drive thru on the way home."

"I wasn't hungry then. I just wanted to go to bed."

"It's good that you got your sleep," Dad said. "And that you're keeping your strength up with food. You're looking a lot better today."

That was the opening I needed. "I'm feeling better. Can I borrow the car? I want to go tell Sarah in person. It doesn't feel right to tell her on the phone."

Mom's hand flew up to her mouth. "She doesn't know."

"None of our friends do. I've decided to tell her first, and then she can help me tell the rest of them." Guilt stabbed me in the gut. They deserved to know about Abby, and I was lying about going to tell them.

"Maybe I should drive you," Mom said.

"No, please, I need a little time to myself before I get there. Just a break before I have to tell her."

"I understand that," Dad said, surprising me. "It's a mental strategy to prepare yourself for a difficult task. It's good for her to learn stress management techniques." He gave Mom a meaningful look.

She relented, still looking worried. "Okay, but text me as soon as you get there. And call us if you need us. It doesn't matter if you drove there. We can still drive you home if you're too upset."

"Okay," I agreed. "Thanks."

I stood and grabbed the car keys before they could change their minds. The doorbell rang as I was about to make my escape.

"Who could that be?" Mom stood and started for the door, with Dad right behind her.

With a sinking feeling that my plans were about to be derailed, I followed them. Mom opened the door and exclaimed in shock. "Devon! What happened?"

Horrified at her reaction, I lunged past her. "Hi! I'm sorry, but I was just leaving." I dangled the keys in front of him as I scanned his expression. He didn't look offended or hurt.

His dark eyes watched me, stirring the butterflies in my stomach. "Where are you going?"

"To a friend's house."

"Really?" he challenged. "Then I'll drive you."

I looked past him and down the driveway. "You've got your truck! I'm so glad he didn't get rid of it."

"My dad was going to go with him on Monday to trade it in and let him pick out whatever car he wanted," he said with a scowl.

"Well, that's all over with now," I said. "I'm sorry, but I really have to go now. I'll talk to you later."

"We'll talk on the way to your friend's house," he countered, fixing a stubborn look on me.

I didn't want to argue with him in front of my parents, so I gave Mom the keys. "Okay, Devon's driving me. See you later."

Luckily, they were too taken aback by him being in a wheelchair again to question my change of plans. Mom, especially, felt bad about how she had reacted. "Text me when you get there," she reminded me in a subdued tone.

"I will," I promised and left with Devon.

As soon as we were in his truck, he said, "I knew you were about to get yourself in trouble."

"Shut up and drive. We're going to Abby's house."

"Hazel," he pleaded, "think about what you're doing. You're going to upset her parents by asking them to let you see their daughter's body."

"That's why I'm going to take them to see Abby first. Then I can explain to them what I want to do."

He gave me a long look, the debate within him clear in his gaze. Shifting it away from me, he closed his eyes and said, "Okay."

CHAPTER 26

didn't dare break the silence on the way to Abby's house. Talking about it could give him a chance to voice his doubt and decide against it. He was clearly torn.

But I had no doubt about this. It would take away her parents' grief, so seeing her body afterwards wouldn't be a problem.

I hopped out of the truck as soon as we pulled into Abby's driveway. Jogging up to the door, I rang the bell and knocked too. Then I rang the bell again.

"Maybe you should give them a chance to get to the door," Devon suggested.

I shifted from foot to foot as I waited, but quickly gave in to my impatience and pounded on the door. "Hello? Is anyone home?" I called out and stabbed at the doorbell for good measure.

The door suddenly opened. "Hazel," Abby's mom exclaimed in surprise.

She looked awful. Her eyes were puffy and red from crying, and her nose was chapped like she'd been blowing it too much. She slouched, holding on to the door like she needed it for support. I would have thought she was sick with the flu if I hadn't known the reason for her suffering.

"We need to talk to you. Can we come in?"

Her gaze shifted to Devon, and her eyes filled with fresh tears. "You saved her last time."

"The doctors saved her. I just called for help."

"Thank you," she said, her voice breaking. "I should have thanked you in person before..."

She stifled a sob, and I rushed forward to hug her. She clung to me and cried. "She's gone. I can't believe she's gone."

"She's actually not. That's why I'm here."

She pulled back from me with a wide-eyed expression of hope. "It was a mistake? Did she wake up at the funeral home?" A horrified look came over her. "Oh, my poor baby!"

"No," I quickly said. "That's not what happened. She's somewhere else."

"They sent her somewhere else?" she asked in bewilderment. "Where?"

"Great job," Devon muttered behind me.

"I'm messing this all up," I acknowledged, but I kept my focus on Abby's mom.

"Where is she? I have to go to her!"

She took a step forward, but I put out a hand to stop her. "We need to sit down first so I can explain it to you."

Since I was already inside, I guided her to the living room couch and sat down with her. She gazed at me expectantly, her demeanor excited and impatient. I glanced at Devon as he approached us, his expression grim and reproachful.

Turning back to Abby's mom, I stalled by asking, "Where's Mr. Collins?"

"He's at the funeral home making the arrangements. I just couldn't do it, so my sister went with him." She frowned. "Why hasn't he called to tell me Abby's not there? Wouldn't they have told him that she never arrived there?"

I took a breath. "I need you to see Abby first before we get into all that." Standing up, I pulled the piece of paper out of my pocket and sat back down. Unfolding it, I said, "Picture Abby as you read this. I mean, really see her in your mind."

She took the paper and skimmed it before looking at me. "What is this?"

"It's a spell. I know it sounds crazy, but it will take us to Abby. I already went and talked to her last night, so I know it works."

The light went out of her eyes as her hope was extinguished. She looked at me with pity. "Oh, sweetheart. I know you can't believe it. I can't either. But magic isn't going to bring her back."

"It won't bring her back, but it will take you to her," Devon said. "Hazel wasn't hallucinating. I've been there myself. It's real."

She assessed him, apparently not sure what to think anymore.

"Please try it and see for yourself," I pleaded. "I'll go with you."

"Go," she repeated with a huffed out little laugh of disbelief. "Okay, sure. Why not?"

"Good. Read the words out loud and really focus on picturing Abby," I instructed.

"I'll stay here," Devon said. "Don't be gone too long. It's gonna be a little hard to explain both of you being passed out if her husband comes home."

"We'll be quick," I promised. Glancing over at Abby's mom, I asked. "Ready?"

Regarding me with a bemused look, she said, "Sure."

Gesturing toward the paper in her hand, I reminded her, "Remember, picture Abby while you read it."

She sighed and then began to speak the words. Despite her doubt, a look of concentration came over her face. A part of her wanted to believe, and that was apparently enough, because she fell back against the couch as she completed the spell.

I didn't waste any time in joining her as I pictured the wall of fog. That was where I found her, staring at it in amazement. She glanced at me, blinking in surprise. "Did you just appear? Because you weren't here a second ago."

"Yes," I said, "so did you. Hold on a minute." I took a breath and yelled, "Lucius! Let us in. I've got Abby's mom with me."

"Come in," he said, sounding annoyed.

I grabbed Mrs. Collins arm and pulled her through the wall with me. She yelped as she stumbled, but then stood staring at Lucius with her mouth open. "You're not in your wheelchair."

"He's not Devon. His name is Lucius."

"His twin? But I thought he..."

Tears sprang to her eyes, but I didn't bother explaining that Lucius wasn't Devon's dead twin. "C'mon," I said, tugging at her arm. "Let's go talk to Abby."

Lucius pivoted and strode away in front of us as we followed. Abby's mom was in a daze as we walked across the drawbridge toward the castle. When we entered, Lucius led us to the dining room. "I shall inform her you are here. Perhaps you can convince her to eat something."

He started for the hallway, but Abby burst into the room at a run. "Mom!"

Her mother cried out at the sight of her and rushed to embrace her. "Abby!

They hugged and cried, and a warm feeling spread through my chest as I watched them. I glanced at Lucius to see his reaction and was pierced by the forlorn expression on his face. He quickly hid it when he noticed me looking at him, and he scowled at me and turned away.

I felt an unwanted pang of sympathy for him though. He'd been here alone for years, and now we were here to take Abby from him. But she shouldn't be stuck here just because he was.

Abby's mom pulled back to look at her. She was dressed in a simple white gown that gave her an angelic appearance.

"Is this heaven?" her mom asked in awe.

Lucius snorted. "Hardly."

"It's an in between place," I said quickly, moving closer to her and Abby. "That's why I need you to let me see her body, so I can try to bring her back."

"Bring her back from the dead?" Lucius asked derisively. "Are you Jesus? Because he's the only one who's supposedly ever done that."

I ignored him and spoke earnestly to Abby's mom. "Will you let me try?"

"Of course," she answered, her voice pepped up with excitement. "If you can save—"

"No!" Abby interjected. "I told you not to do that. I don't want to be some evil thing brought back with creepy magic like in Pet Cemetery."

"It's not any kind of magic or spell," I told her. "I'll use my power.

Like I did to get here. I didn't have to use a spell, just the power of my mind."

"Which means you're harnessing your power," Lucius said. "That's good, Hazel. You should be developing it. But you have only just begun, and I doubt even an experienced practitioner could raise the dead."

"Meaning that you can't, so you don't think I can either," I shot back. "But I can do things you can't."

Reaching out to touch Abby's dress, I closed my eyes and imagined it being the same sky blue as her eyes. I heard her mom gasp, and looked to see that it was now the way I had envisioned it.

I smiled in triumph. "See? I've got this."

Pointing a finger at Abby, I said, "Eat something. I don't want you fainting as soon as you get back."

She glanced down at her gown and then at me. "You have magic powers," she said in awe.

"That doesn't mean she can do anything," Lucius grumbled.

But I was riding high on a surge of confidence. I'd succeeded in bringing Abby's mom here and making them both happy when they'd been so sad. Everything was working out the way I wanted, and I was sure I could fix this final thing.

"We have to go," I said. "Be ready to get back in your body."

Abby appeared hopeful now, but her mom didn't want to leave. "Can't I stay here with her until you bring her back?"

"They won't let me see her body without your permission, and your husband probably won't believe me."

Her face fell. "You're right. I didn't believe you until I saw her for myself."

With a sigh, she moved in to give Abby another hug. This time, there were no tears, since they expected to see each other again.

"Where's the spell?" I asked, seeing that Abby's mom was no longer holding it in her hand.

"Oh! I think I dropped it outside when I got here. I'm sorry. I was so surprised to be somewhere else all of a sudden."

"I'll get it," Lucius said and disappeared.

Abby and her mom both gasped. He was back before we could get over the shock, startling all of us with his reappearance. He had the piece of paper and tried to hand it to Abby's mom, but she backed away from him.

I snatched it and tried to soothe her. "It's okay. It's a magic thing just like me changing the color of Abby's dress."

She stared at me. "Can you do that too?"

"We both did it to get here," I pointed out. "We appeared here out of nowhere, right?"

"Well, yes, I guess so."

I moved on from that. "Anyway, now you need to picture your living room to get back. Say the words and imagine yourself there."

She cast a last look at Abby, who smiled encouragingly at her. Glancing down at the paper, she read the spell aloud and vanished.

"I'll bring you back," I told Abby and transported myself to her house.

CHAPTER 27

Devon drove us to the funeral home. Abby's mom sat beside him in the front seat, since offering it to her had seemed like the polite thing to do. A weird mix of energy filled the cab of the truck. Peace and serenity flowed from Abby's mom as she gazed out the windshield. Beside her, Devon radiated tension with the rigid set of his shoulders. I sat in the back practically vibrating with impatience and anticipation.

This was it, and all of us knew it. We were just approaching it in different ways, but it was happening. We said nothing when we arrived and followed Abby's mom inside.

"I need to see my daughter's body," she told the attendant who greeted her.

A startled expression flitted over the woman's face before it settled into a polite mask. "Have you spoken to anyone about arrangements yet?"

"My husband is here speaking to them now, but I just need to see my daughter's body."

The woman's eyes held a hint of wariness, but she kept her composure. "What is her name?"

"Abigail Collins."

"One moment while I get someone to help you."

She went and knocked on an office door, going inside and closing it behind her. Worry had crept in to make me nervous. It hadn't occurred to me that they might not let us see Abby's body, but that awkward exchange wasn't giving me confidence.

We didn't wait long before the door opened, and Abby's dad strode out with the attendant right behind him. Abby's aunt and a man in a suit followed them.

"Honey, what are you doing here?" Mr. Collins asked in concern, moving in to put his arm around his wife. "I thought you were staying home to rest."

She smiled up at him. "I'm okay now. Hazel needs to see Abby's body. I'll explain it all later, but we have to do this."

"I'm sorry," the man in the suit said. "But she hasn't been prepared for viewing. If you'll join us in my office, we can—"

"No," she interrupted, moving out from under her husband's arm to face off against the man. "I am her mother, and I have the right to see her. Take us to her right now."

Abby's aunt stepped forward, trying to soothe her. "Nicole, don't do this to yourself. Let me take you home, and—"

"No," she interrupted again, standing firm. "Hazel needs to see her. It's important."

"Honey," her husband said, "you know that's not a good idea. You know how hard it was for us." Tears sprang to his eyes as he got choked up, but he cleared his throat and continued. "Hazel shouldn't see her like that."

"I need to. Please! It's important."

He shook his head. "You might think that, but you'll regret it. It's better when it doesn't feel real, believe me."

"You don't understand," I began, but his wife grabbed his attention away from me.

She faced him and looked into his eyes. "If you love me, if you love Abby, you will do this for us. I need you to trust me on this. Please, because I'll never forgive you if you don't."

I held my breath as we all waited for his decision.

He stared at her and then said, "I'll make a deal with you. I'll do it if you stay here with Lisa. Hazel can go with me."

"But I want to be there when—"

"It's fine!" I exclaimed, fearful that she had been about to say *when she opens her eyes*. "I'll go with him."

Her sheepish expression told me that I'd been right. "Okay, I'll wait here."

"Steve," the man in the suit said, apparently knowing Abby's dad well enough to call him by his first name. "You know this isn't protocol."

With the hard edge of authority in his voice, he replied, "Parental rights take precedence over your protocol. Take us to her, Jeff."

Jeff apparently thought better of arguing with a police officer. "Alright." He pulled out his phone and stepped away from us, but I still heard what he said. "Set Miss Collins out for examination. I'll be there shortly."

He came back to us with a grim expression. "Come with me."

"See you in a little while," Abby's mom said, sounding cheerful.

Her husband shot her a concerned look. "We'll be back soon."

He glanced at Devon as we started down the hallway. "What are you doing?"

"Going with Hazel," he replied. "She needs me there."

A look of understanding passed between them, and Mr. Collins gave him a nod. I knew that Devon meant for moral support, but I hoped he'd change his mind and combine his power with mine to help me bring Abby back. Either way, his presence did give me a boost.

I was so glad he was back here with me. We just needed Abby, and everything would be set right. Life would return to normal, and hopefully the rest of senior year would be much better from here on out. I was lost in my thoughts and didn't pay attention to where we were going, but I was roused from my reverie when we stopped.

We'd come to a door, but instead of opening it, the man pulled out his phone again. "I need masks and shields for four people."

When the door cracked open, someone from inside handed him the supplies, which he passed around to us. I was surprised that we had to put on both masks to cover our mouths and noses and face shields over that. It was only Abby, and she wasn't contaminated with some kind of biohazard or anything.

But I wasn't prepared for the sight of her. The unnatural pallor of her skin and her completely lifeless form left no doubt that she was dead. Even worse, her body was laid out on a blue tarp on top of what looked like an autopsy table.

"Ew, gross," Abby said, and I nearly jumped out of my skin. "I didn't look this bad yesterday."

I turned my head to see her standing next to a cabinet—where there had been no one just seconds ago. She was looking at the body on the table in disgust.

"Are you okay?" her dad asked me, unaware that the ghost of his daughter was in the room with us. "Do you need to leave?"

"Did they have to leave me in that ugly hospital gown?" Abby complained. "What happened to my dress?"

She didn't look like a ghost. Not transparent or anything like that. But she was standing here outside of her dead body, so she had to be a ghost. I wondered if Svetlana had looked like this, like a regular person. No wonder I hadn't been afraid of her.

"I'm okay," I said, knowing that they would think I was crazy if I told them what was happening.

"I told you this was a bad idea," Devon said. "You shouldn't be—"

"I'm fine," I cut in. "We're here, and I'm doing this."

It didn't seem like he knew Abby was here, but I couldn't be sure with him.

"Doing what?" Abby's dad asked. "You said you needed to see her, and you have. There's no reason for you to be here any longer."

He was doing the strong cop thing, but I could tell that this was hard on him. He was avoiding looking at Abby's body, and I knew that he really wanted to leave.

I didn't want to prolong this for him, but it would be worth it if I could bring her back. Having Abby here had taken away the horror of her dead body for me, but I still wanted to get this done as quickly as possible.

"I need to say goodbye to her. Please give me a little more time."

I couldn't see his expression, but above his mask, his eyes were sad. "Do what you need to do."

Abby had moved closer to him. She tried to touch his arm, but her hand went right through it. She stared at it in astonishment.

But I didn't have time to watch her right now. I had to focus my energy on her body. Stepping closer to it, I concentrated on gathering my power in preparation for unleashing it.

"Don't touch the body," the man said, breaking my concentration.

I shot him an annoyed look. "I won't. Please don't interrupt me."

Focusing again, I pictured the lifeless form in front of me regaining health and vitality. The power inside me coalesced, but I hesitated to unleash it all at once. What if I accidentally torched Abby's body instead of restoring it?

So, I let the energy slowly flow out of me, and I could feel it going somewhere amazing. It was working, because I was more alive than I'd ever been. I traveled past stars and planets, because I was free and limitless.

Until I was yanked back into my body. My weak and drained body that was being lifted by strong arms. "What's happening?"

"You fainted," Abby's dad said as he carried me toward the door. "Jeff, get the boy. He passed out too."

"I'm okay," Devon said. "I've got it."

"But Abby. Check her pulse."

"Thank God you're okay," she said, coming up beside us with an anxious expression.

My heart sank at the sight of her, because she was ghost Abby in her blue gown from the castle.

Jeff rushed through her to open the door for us. I heard the sound of zipping behind us, along with a crinkling sound. I put the clues together and had the horrible realization that Abby hadn't been laid out on a tarp.

It was a body bag, and they were closing her up in it. Because she was still dead.

I'd failed.

I stared at Abby in disbelief as her dad carried me out into the hall-way. She hadn't come back to life.

What were we going to do now?

CHAPTER 28

"You look worse than when you were in a coma," Abby said.

"Thanks," I muttered.

"For saving your life? No problem," Devon said. "It's not like you could have had the sense to stop when you realized you were dying."

"Dying?" Abby and I exclaimed simultaneously.

He glanced over at me but quickly returned his eyes to the road. We were alone in his truck, since Abby's mom had gone home with her husband. He'd wanted to take me to the hospital because I was still so weak, but he'd been distracted by his wife breaking down in tears when I'd had to admit, "It didn't work."

Devon had taken the opportunity to lie that he was taking me to the hospital, and he'd told me to sit on his lap and given me a ride out to his truck. I'd needed it too, because I couldn't have walked out of there on my own. I was that depleted of energy that I could barely stand when Abby's dad set me down to attend to his wife.

"Didn't you feel your life draining out of you?" Devon demanded. "Because I sure did. I called out to you and tried to shake you out of it, but you didn't listen."

"You did? I wasn't aware of any of that. I thought it was working because I felt so alive."

Slumping in my seat, I added, "I don't understand what happened."

He was quiet for a minute but then cast another glance at me. "What was that place?"

I perked up. "You saw it too?"

"Yeah, when I came after you. Planets and stars like we were out in space."

"Wasn't it amazing?"

"But what was it? Where were we?"

An idea formed in my mind, and I asked quietly, "Are you sure that I was dying?"

He glanced at me again and scoffed. "Heaven? You think you can just visit it anytime you feel like it?"

"You said yourself that I was dying," I reminded him. "And I don't think it was heaven. I felt like I was going somewhere, but you stopped me before I got there."

"Oh my God!" Abby exclaimed. "You really almost died because of me."

"No, I didn't. He's exaggerating."

"Oh yeah? What would have happened if he hadn't come after you? You said you were going to heaven."

"I don't know that for sure," I began.

"Who are you talking to?" Devon asked, shooting me a look.

"So, you really don't see her or hear her," I mused.

"Who?"

"Abby. She's in the backseat."

"Oh, I thought you can only follow your body around." He winced as soon as he said it. "Um, that's what I was limited to when Lucius was using mine."

"Because he wasn't dead," Abby concluded. "I'm a ghost, Hazel, right? I'm really dead," she added, getting upset.

I turned to look at her, but she was gone. "Abby?"

With a heavy sigh, I faced forward. "She left. She's probably going back there to cry. I can't believe I screwed it all up so bad."

"You didn't screw up anything. What you were trying to do is impossible."

I leaned my head against the window. "I just need to get my strength back, and I'll try again. If at first you don't—"

My words cut off as he swerved into a fast-food parking lot. My seat-belt tightened across my chest and kept me in place as he slammed on the brakes. His seatbelt snapped back into its holder as he undid it in a hurry.

Leaning in close to my face, he said, "You almost *died*. Get it? If I hadn't stopped you, you would have been *dead*."

I blinked at him, processing his words and rejecting them.

He scowled and spoke in a harsher tone. "You would have ended up in your own body bag."

The image was so horrific that it got through to me. I shuddered as I imagined it being zipped up over my face, and a sob escaped me as I remembered the sound of it being zipped up over Abby.

Devon released my seatbelt and pulled me into his arms. I clung to him and cried as I realized that my best friend was dead for real. I couldn't bring her back to life. We weren't going to spend the rest of senior year together and go to the same college. We wouldn't be bridesmaids at each other's weddings like we'd planned since we were little girls. Abby would never even have a wedding. She would never get to fall in love. Her entire future was gone.

I pulled back and wiped my eyes. "Will you take me to Sarah's house?" I asked somberly. "I need to tell her about Abby."

"Maybe you should get checked out at the hospital first," he said. "We're almost there."

My mouth dropped open. "You were really driving me to the hospital? I thought you just said that to Mr. Collins to get him to leave us alone."

"Why are you still not getting it?" he demanded. "You almost died, Hazel. You need to take that seriously."

"I am," I insisted. "But I'm okay now. I don't need to go to the hospital."

He gave me a skeptical look, but he relented. "Give me the address to Sarah's house."

I did, and then realized I should text her to make sure she was home. She texted back that I should come over, and that she couldn't wait to hear about the party.

I winced, dreading breaking the news to her, but knowing I had to.

I'd been hoping that we'd be visiting Abby in the hospital after her miraculous recovery instead, but that hadn't happened.

The only positive was that I'd regained some of my strength by the time we arrived, so I was able to walk up to Sarah's door. She answered it with a big smile, but it slipped off her face when she saw Devon.

She stared at him in dismay. "What happened? I thought you were cured."

"I didn't have a disease," he muttered before his expression softened. "Hazel needs to tell you something."

He turned his attention to me. "Call me when you need me to drive you home. I'll leave you guys to talk."

He spun around and glided back to his truck. I watched him, partly because my eyes were drawn to him and partly to put off what I had to do.

"Oh my God, I was so rude," Sarah exclaimed. "I was just so surprised to see him back in his wheelchair. Should I ask him to come in?"

She started to step outside, but I put up my hand to stop her. "Let him go. I have to talk to you."

"About what happened to him?" she asked, glancing toward him as he got into his truck.

I took a breath. "No. About what happened to Abby."

After the disbelief and the tears, Sarah texted the rest of our friends to come over. We went through it all over again with them and ended up having a weird sleepover. It was comforting to be together in our grief, but I conked out before the others were even thinking about going to sleep.

I slept straight through until dawn, having been out since late afternoon the previous day. The last thing I remembered was Sarah's mom ordering pizza for us, but it hadn't arrived before I'd apparently dozed off on the sofa.

I got up quietly, careful not to wake Kyle, who was stretched out on the recliner across from me.

After all those hours, I really needed to pee, so I made my way to the bathroom. Once I was done and had washed my hands, I realized that sleeping had restored my energy. I no longer felt weak and drained, and I had scurried down the hall on steady legs. I was physically back to normal, and I was glad that I had talked Devon out of taking me to the hospital and worrying my parents for nothing.

I was also glad that they hadn't seen me in my weakened state yesterday. I'd only had to talk to my mom on the phone when I'd called to tell her that I was staying the night here. If I had sounded off to her, she hadn't mentioned it. She'd said that it was good for me to be with my friends, and she'd been right. There was comfort in it, even though it didn't change what had happened. Grieving together was better than grieving alone.

But Devon was alone. When I'd texted him to tell him I didn't need a ride home, I couldn't invite him to join us, since it wasn't my house. He hadn't known Abby very well, so he wasn't as affected by her death as we were. But he had been in that room with me with her dead body. That hadn't been easy to see, and he shouldn't be handling everything on his own.

But that's what he'd been doing ever since his accident. He was tough and strong, but having no friends had to suck. I was going to try my best to draw him into our group.

I went outside and listened to the birds chirping as I enjoyed the early morning peace. It was Sunday, so most people weren't up yet. I hadn't done this in years, but I loved the start of a new day when I didn't have to rush to school. It was hard to believe that Abby would never get to experience this again.

"Oh my God, Hazel," she said, making me jump with her sudden appearance. "Do you know what my mom did? She brought my dad to the castle! He's gotta think he's losing his mind. You know how he's all about facts and evidence. I know he humored her doing that spell with her, thinking it wasn't gonna work. You should have seen his face."

I shrugged. "I was going to bring him with us too, but he wasn't home when I brought your mom to see you."

She gaped at me. "My dad's a cop, and you thought that was a good idea."

"What? It's not illegal. You're not committing a crime."

"Hazel, you don't get it. This has messed up his mind. He doesn't know what to think anymore. How's he supposed to go back to normal life now? My mom's different, because seeing me helped her to deal with me dying."

"It had to help him too," I insisted. "This isn't some case he's trying to solve. He's your *dad*. It doesn't matter if he doesn't understand it. Knowing that you're okay is all he'll care about. Especially after what I put him through yesterday. I'm so sorry I couldn't bring you back!"

She gave me a disapproving look. "I told you not to try. You're so lucky I didn't turn into a zombie, because you guys were closed up with me in that room. You probably wouldn't have made it out alive."

She pointed her finger at me accusingly. "You almost didn't. Don't ever do that again!"

"But now I know what to look out for. Maybe if—"

"No!" she exclaimed, glaring at me. "Don't you dare. It's my body, and I'm telling you no. I mean it, Hazel. I'll never speak to you again."

I deflated. "Okay, if that's what you want. But I hate to give up."

"It's not giving up. It's accepting reality. You can't bring people back from death."

"What's the point of even having this power if I can't use it to help you?" I complained in frustration.

"But you *are* helping me. Nobody else can see me or talk to me when I'm here, but you can. I can still talk to my best friend, and that helps a lot." She smiled at me. "It still feels the same with you, like nothing's changed."

I smiled back at her. "It does when I talk to you like this. I was just thinking that you can't experience the morning with the birds chirping, but you can, because you're here with me now."

She looked across the lawn and out at the quiet street as we stood there listening to the birds for a bit. "It's so peaceful. I can't remember the last time I did this," she commented.

"Hazel, there you are," a voice behind us said.

I turned to see Sarah's mom approaching. "Just enjoying the birds."

Abby snickered, and I shot her a look. Her expression quickly turned serious. "Don't act like you see someone she can't, or you'll look like a crazy person. I should go back anyway. See you."

She disappeared, and I was left to deal with this strange new reality where my best friend was dead but wasn't.

CHAPTER 29

Abby's funeral was weird. Mostly because she was there commenting on the whole thing.

"Look at that faker. She called me a boring nobody two days before I died, and now she's pretending like she's heartbroken."

Since no one else could see or hear her, I couldn't react to anything she was saying. I tried to keep a neutral expression on my face, but that was probably strange to people too, since I was supposed to be sad about my best friend.

"Aww, that guy I was talking to at the party is here. That's so sweet."

I got out my phone and typed in my notes, holding it so she could see it. "He tried to save me? I wish I could give him a hug."

But she couldn't. Although she looked solid to me, she couldn't hug me either. She was a ghost in this world, walking around unseen among the people here to mourn her. I hadn't told her parents about this. It was enough for them to know that she was alive in Lucius's world.

At least I thought she was alive. I wasn't sure how she could be when her body was dead. But Lucius had never even had a body in this world, and he must be alive if he aged. Ghosts never got any older, because they remained the age they'd been when they died. It was too early to tell with Abby. I would watch to see if she changed over time.

"What?" she exclaimed in shock. "He's here? How did he know?"

I followed the direction of her gaze and saw a guy who looked slightly familiar walking into the room. "Who?" I risked asking, since it was only one word.

"My brother. I sent him a message, but I didn't tell him how we were connected. I just said I needed to talk to him about something important about his dad."

I started toward him, because he looked hesitant to walk in further.

"Oh, hell no!" Abby exclaimed. "I don't want *him* here. I can't believe he had the nerve to show up."

The man showed no hesitation at all as he gestured for his son to follow him. There was no doubt that he was Abby's biological father, because she looked a lot like him. They had the same blond hair and sky-blue eyes. But while Abby was pretty, this man had movie star looks.

He also had the ego to match. Cutting in front of people who were waiting to give their condolences to Abby's parents, he strode right up to them. "How dare you not tell me about my daughter's funeral," I heard him say as I moved closer.

"Oh, did you finally remember you have a daughter?" Abby's mom retorted. "How convenient that you care when it's too late to be a father to her."

"You tell him, Mom," Abby exclaimed, clearly enjoying this.

"Hi, I'm Jacob Lind," her brother interjected. "I'm so sorry for your loss."

Abby's mom looked from him to her ex-husband. "You have a son?"

He puffed up with pride. "Yes, he's my boy."

She regarded him with disdain. "And it never occurred to you to tell her that she has a brother?"

Jacob cast his father a resentful look before saying, "I just found out about it myself. Abby messaged me on Instagram but didn't tell me who she was. When she didn't reply to my message, I went back to her profile and saw the posts from her friends. I'm so sorry. I wish I could have met her."

"I should have contacted him sooner. He seems nice," Abby said sadly.

"Thank you," her mom told him. "I'm sure she would have loved to meet you."

He gave her a sad smile and circled back to Abby's coffin instead of skipping it altogether like I'd thought he would. Abby went to stand beside him as he gazed at her body with regret on his face.

When he walked away after bowing his head, I went up to him and introduced myself. "Hi, I'm Hazel. I'm Abby's best friend. She told me about you."

His expression brightened, and I saw his resemblance to Abby. "She did?"

"Yes. She was surprised that she had a brother." I omitted the part about her being jealous of him.

"I wish I knew about her sooner. I always wanted a brother or sister," he said wistfully.

"We *would* have known if his father wasn't such an asshole," Abby said.

Proving her point, the man was ready to leave already. "Let's go, Jacob. We're not wanted here anyway," he sniffed.

His son leveled a hostile stare on him. "I'm staying. You go home if you want. I'll call Mom to come get me later." He strode off to look at the display of pictures showcasing Abby's life, and she followed him.

His father huffed in exasperation and went to sit in the very back row of chairs that had been set out. I walked out into the hallway and jotted down my number on a memorial card. Going back into the viewing room, I found Jacob still perusing the photos.

Handing the card to him, I said, "You can text me or call me if you have any questions about Abby."

"Thanks," he told me. "I'd like to know as much as I can about her, but I don't want to bother her parents."

"He's so sweet," Abby said in amazement. "How did he have such a sweet kid?"

"You're sweet too," I reminded her.

Jacob thought I was talking to him and got bashful. "I...uh, I'll call you."

"My little brother has a crush on you," Abby trilled. "How cute is that?"

I gave him an embarrassed smile and went to pay my final respects to Abby.

She walked up to the casket with me. "They did pretty good with the makeup. I still look dead, but not as awful as before. I don't know how you weren't scared to try to bring me back. That whole thing was like a scene from a horror movie when the corpse is about to open its eyes and attack everyone."

I found it impossible to feel sad with her standing right next to me making comments like that. "This is supposed to be a serious moment," I said, taking the opportunity to respond to her without looking like I was talking to myself. It was acceptable to talk to a dead person in this situation.

"I'm seriously annoyed with my mom for not putting me in the dress I wanted. I looked so much better in it than this church outfit. She said it would be morbid for me to be in the dress I died in. Hello, this is a funeral. It's already morbid."

I gave up and just said, "I love you, Abby."

"Aww, I love you too, Hazel."

I walked over to her parents and said, "I'm so sorry for your loss."

Abby's mom gave me a hug. "Thank you for your help. I couldn't have made it through this without seeing her."

She couldn't elaborate with other people around, but I knew she meant seeing Abby at the castle. I'd thought she'd be upset with me for not bringing Abby back.

To my surprise, Abby's dad also hugged me. "She told me what you tried to do," he said quietly into my ear, "and how you almost died."

He pulled back, his eyes brimming with emotion. "I'm sorry. Taking you there was…"

He shook his head. "I had to be out of my mind. I'm so sorry, Hazel."

"No," I said, trying to convey how much I meant it. "Thank you for doing that. I wanted to try. I *had* to try. I'm sorry it didn't work."

"I'm not," Abby said. "I still say you would have turned me into a zombie."

I almost rolled my eyes, but that would have been extremely inappropriate.

"Oh, Hazel, that's just not possible," her dad said. "I understand your wishful thinking, but you have to know that there was nothing you could do. Don't beat yourself up over it."

"Okay," I agreed, although a part of me still wondered if I could have done something differently.

My parents approached, and I drifted away while they were giving their condolences to Abby's parents. I spotted Devon entering the room, and my heart lifted. Hurrying over to him, I greeted him with an enthusiastic, "Hi!"

His eyes warmed, but he replied dryly, "You should probably tone down the smile. It'll be weird for people to see you looking so happy."

"Oh, right," I said, glancing at Abby. "Sorry."

"Actually, it would be fun to see everyone's reactions if you did something really inappropriate," she said with a mischievous smile. "Like kiss him on the mouth. Really go for it with tongue and everything."

"Abby!" I screeched, my cheeks going hot with embarrassment.

She laughed and pointed at me. "You should see your face."

"Hazel," Devon snapped.

I froze, realizing what I'd just done. I'd shrieked out Abby's name, forgetting that she was dead and not visible to anyone else. I shrank into myself as I noticed the people standing nearby staring at me. Luckily, there was enough chatter that my voice hadn't been heard by everyone in the large room.

Still, I retreated into the hallway and went outside. Devon followed me.

"What did she say to make you react like that?" he asked when we were out of earshot of other people.

I waved it off. "Nothing."

"You know what else would be fun? If I could move stuff around and freak everyone out. What's the point of being a ghost if you can't scare anyone?"

"Now she wishes she could move things and scare people," I told him. "I don't know why she'd want to do that," I added, giving her the side eye.

His gaze filled with compassion. "Because it sucks to be somewhere but not be a part of it. All you can do is watch, while no one even knows you're there. You want to shake them and yell in their faces, but they can't hear you. It's very frustrating. I get why you want to scare them, Abby. I'm sorry I can't hear you or see you either. But at least Hazel can."

Abby looked confused. "When was he a ghost? He was never dead."

"No, but he could see what Lucius was doing when he was in his body."

Her face paled. "What? I thought he was stuck in the other world."

"He was, because he couldn't return to his body. But he could be there outside of his body somehow." I frowned at her. "What's wrong?"

She looked horrified. "He was there the entire time Lucius was in his body?"

"No. He would go check on him and come back."

"Oh. So, um, what kind of stuff did he see?"

"Just him talking with his dad," I said with a dismissive wave, not wanting to get into it in front of Devon.

She looked at Devon, trying to read him. He'd been waiting patiently while we talked, but his expression had hardened when I mentioned his father. He hadn't wanted to discuss him at all since he'd returned.

"We should get back inside before your parents come looking for you," he said.

They had become more concerned about me than ever. Since the doctor had wrongly assumed that my coma had been caused by stress, they worried that Abby's death would overload me with it.

Maybe I would have been devastated to the point of breaking if she was really gone and I could never see her again. Not that this wasn't hard, because it was. She wouldn't be at school with me anymore and having lunch with me in the cafeteria. She couldn't go have fun with our friends. Like Devon had pointed out, she couldn't participate in anything anymore. She was going to miss out on so much.

I held back my tears, because I didn't want to make Abby sad. She'd been handling her funeral amazingly well, and I wasn't going to drag down her mood. She was silent as we went back inside, casting speculative looks at Devon that I couldn't ask her about in front of him.

My parents met us in the hallway, relief on their faces when they saw me. "There you are," Mom said. She turned her attention to Devon and gave him a sad smile. "Hello, Devon."

"Hi, Mrs. Guthrie. Mr. Guthrie. If you'll excuse me, I need to go pay my respects." With a nod at them, he glided down the hall into the viewing room.

"Poor boy," Mom said sadly. "Such a shame his recovery didn't last. It must be so hard on him."

"He's fine," I snapped, tired of her constantly feeling sorry for him. She hadn't reacted that way when she first met him. She'd accepted him the way he was.

"Hazel, put yourself in his shoes." She cringed at her choice of words but went on. "Imagine regaining the ability to walk only to lose it again. It has to be devastating."

She didn't know that had been a different person—if Lucius was actually a person. But Devon *had* been able to walk in his world. It didn't bother me that he was back in his wheelchair, but maybe it bothered him. I didn't want to think about this.

Devon was back, and Lucius was gone. That was a win, and we needed to be grateful for every win. Because we'd had a huge loss.

A loss that I couldn't help noticing was once again connected to me. First my boyfriend, Matt. Now my best friend, Abby. Who would be next?

"I'm going to find my friends," I said, moving to escape my unwanted thoughts.

Abby went with me to where our friends stood together in a group. They greeted me with somber faces as they took turns hugging me.

"I still can't believe it," Sarah said, beginning to cry.

"I'll see you later," Abby told me and vanished.

I'd been right that seeing her friends cry would be too much for her. It was better that she wasn't here for this anyway.

"It's so unfair that she's gone, when there are bad people living until they're old," Kyle said bitterly.

"Abby is in heaven," Emily said. "It's sad for us, but she's happy."

Her words hit me like a ton of bricks. Abby wasn't happy. She was dead, but she wasn't in heaven. She was stuck in Lucius's world, because he'd urged her to go there.

And I'd helped him.

I seethed in anger while my friends grieved. I'd wanted to draw Devon into our group, but I could barely interact with them myself. He noticed my change in mood, but I shook my head when he gave me a questioning look.

I held his hand though when it was time to take our seats for the service. I sat right next to the aisle so he could be beside me in his wheel-chair. His presence couldn't calm me, but it sustained me as I pretended to listen to the preacher talk.

Finally, it was over, and we were going home. We all stood up, and I was first to step into the aisle. Impulsively, I leaned down to kiss Devon. It was a tender kiss rather than the passionate kiss Abby had suggested.

Pulling back and gazing into his eyes, I said, "I love you."

Intense emotion stared back at me from the dark depths of his eyes. "I love you, Hazel."

Magic arced between us, giving me strength for the battle ahead.

CHAPTER 30

had to run the gauntlet of questions from my parents first. They had been seated on the other side of me and had heard my declaration of love to Devon.

"You love him?" Mom asked as soon as we were in the car. "Didn't you just start dating him?"

Dad was more concerned with the kiss. "Don't you think it was inappropriate to kiss him at a funeral? That was disrespectful to Abby's parents, and to their daughter's memory. How could you be thinking about a boy at a time like that?"

I couldn't tell him that Abby would have approved. "Abby would have been happy for me," I said instead. "She knew that I've had a crush on him for a long time."

"How long?" Mom questioned.

"Since the first day of high school," I replied. "It was love at first sight."

"That's infatuation," Dad said dismissively. "You can't love someone you don't know."

"But it never went away. Even when I was dating Matt," I admitted. "I think it's destiny for us to be together."

Dad scoffed. "You're in high school. That's not destiny. It's just limited choices. You'll meet lots of new guys after you graduate and go to college."

He frowned. "College guys might not be the best choice either. When you start your career, you'll meet serious, responsible guys."

"How romantic," I said sarcastically.

"You're too young to know if it's true love," Mom interjected. "Your head is full of romantic notions that might not stand the test of time. All we're saying is to take it slow and make sure it's real."

"If a guy tells you he loves you right away, he's probably only after one thing," Dad added and cleared his throat.

I could have told him that I'd already turned down sex with Devon, but I didn't think that would endear him to my dad. It was too bad that I couldn't tell him how Devon had saved my life, and how he'd risked his own life in order to come find me in Lucius's world. How he'd known that Lucius wanted to steal his body, and he'd left it for me anyway. So that I could go back to mine.

He'd put me first, and wasn't that proof that he loved me?

"I'm not going to sleep with him, if that's what you're worried about," I said, hoping to put his mind to rest. "I've got more important things going on right now."

That *did* seem to convince him. He expelled a heavy breath. "You have too much to deal with at your age. It will be good for you to talk to someone about it. Doctor Barlow will help you sort it all out."

"And talking to your friends will help too. You can also talk to us," Mom added. "I hope you know we're always here for you."

"I do," I said, meaning it.

But the one I needed to talk to wasn't in this world. I bided my time, having a bowl of cereal when we got home. Eating something always convinced my mom that I was okay.

"I'm going to bed," I told her. "I'm wiped out."

"Yes, it's been an exhausting day," she agreed, but she looked concerned.

"Goodnight," I said and went upstairs to my room. I changed into my sleep clothes and lay down to wait.

Closing my eyes when I heard the footsteps in the hall, I pretended to be asleep. My door quietly opened, and I knew that Mom was checking on me. I lay still for a moment, and then rolled to my side so she'd know I wasn't in a coma.

The door quietly shut, and I waited several moments before getting up and changing into jeans and a t-shirt. I wasn't going to face off against Lucius in my pajamas. At the last minute, I remembered to put on my shoes. Arriving in socks would undermine my message. He needed to take me seriously.

Laying back down on my bed, I pictured where I wanted to go and was instantly there. The mystical wall in front of me wouldn't stop me, and my seething anger propelled me through it.

"Lucius!" I yelled as I stormed toward the castle.

He appeared right in front of me, and I shrieked in fright as I almost walked into him. His calm composure while I stood there panting with my hand pressed to my racing heart infuriated me.

"You asshole," I exclaimed as I smacked his arm.

"You called for me, did you not?"

I huffed, hating that he'd thrown me off balance and ruined my entrance. But he was also pissing me off even more, and I'd come here for a confrontation. And this wasn't about me.

"You kept Abby from going to heaven," I accused, my eyes burning with sudden, unshed tears.

I'd startled him out of his cool demeanor. "What?"

I stabbed my finger into his chest. "You tricked her into coming here. She was supposed to go to heaven. How could you do that to her?"

He scowled at me. "I saved her life. What kind of a friend are you that you would want her dead?"

"You *didn't* save her life. She died! I was just at the funeral home where her body is. She can't go back to it and be alive."

"But she's alive here. It's preferable to not existing at all."

"She wouldn't stop existing. She'd be in heaven if you hadn't kept her from going there."

He scoffed. "That's a story for children. There is no evidence that such a place exists."

"I saw it!"

He stared at me. "You saw heaven?"

"Well, maybe not heaven," I amended. "But I went someplace when I was dying. It was amazing, with planets and stars. But I was still headed somewhere before Devon pulled me back. I think I might have been on my way to heaven."

He searched my eyes, looking for deceit. "You could have been hallucinating," he suggested, but he sounded uncertain for the first time since I'd known him.

"I wasn't," I said with complete certainty. "It was real."

His unexpected ignorance of what he'd done made me change tactics. I'd thought he'd done it on purpose to…

Well, I wasn't sure why. But since it hadn't been deliberate, I now had hope that he would help me fix this. "We have to find a way to set her free."

He frowned. "Set her free?"

"Abby. She needs to go to heaven."

His eyebrows lifted. "You've come here to kill her?"

I recoiled. "Of course not! I meant we could do a spell or something."

"To kill her."

"No," I exclaimed in frustration. "To set her soul free."

He sighed. "Haven't you learned by now not to meddle in such things? You nearly died trying to resurrect her body. Your energy was draining so quickly that I thought it was already too late."

"Wait, you were there?"

"Yes, he was there, so I could be as well. I wanted to see you perform this miracle," he added sarcastically.

My eyes narrowed on him. "*You* kept it from working. You wanted me to fail."

His expression hardened. "You think I didn't want you to succeed? I did everything I could to save her."

"You trapped her here. Just like you tried to trap Devon here."

"I *did* trap him. I'd won. I had the life that rightfully belonged to me, but I gave it up to save Abby. This world was crumbling without me, and she would have perished if I hadn't returned."

He looked at me with cold bitterness. "Go and enjoy your victory with that wretch. Be gone from here. I forbid you to return."

I opened my mouth to tell him that he couldn't forbid me, but I was back home in my bed. Annoyed, I pictured the castle, but I remained where I was. I tried picturing the house instead, but that didn't work either.

He couldn't really keep me from going there, could he?

Getting worried now, I pictured Abby and was transported to the dark, deserted funeral home. Abby's casket was closed now, and it was creepy being here by myself. I quickly returned to my bedroom.

What was I going to do now?

I couldn't leave Abby trapped in Lucius's world, but he'd kicked me out and wasn't letting me back in. It was a bit ironic when I'd been so desperate to escape from there before.

I stewed in anger and frustration as I thought about everything. We'd finally gotten rid of Lucius from our lives, but now he had Abby. I had to find a way to set her free. Wincing as I recalled Lucius saying that meant killing her, I reminded myself that she was already dead.

This would be the same thing that I'd done for Svetlana. I'd be helping her move on to a better place. It would definitely be a better place than where she was now.

She had no one there, and it was cruel of Lucius to keep me from visiting her. I was going to get revenge on him for that. Maybe I'd disintegrate him into ashes like I done to the monsters. If Devon and I combined our power, we could do it.

I couldn't do anything tonight, and Abby's funeral was tomorrow. But after that, I was going to work with Devon to fix this. We weren't done fighting Lucius yet.